Magic Diary

PAT LaMARCHE

MILFORD HOUSE

Milford House Press
Mechanicsburg, Pennsylvania

MILFORD HOUSE

an imprint of Sunbury Press, Inc.
Mechanicsburg, PA USA

For information about special discounts for bulk purchases, please contact Sunbury Press Orders Dept. at (855) 338-8359 or orders@sunburypress.com.

To request one of our authors for speaking engagements or book signings, please contact Sunbury Press Publicity Dept. at publicity@sunburypress.com.

ISBN: 978-1-62006-172-5 (Trade paperback)

Library of Congress Control Number:

FIRST MILFORD HOUSE PRESS EDITION: June 2019

Product of the United States of America
0 1 1 2 3 5 8 13 21 34 55

Set in Bookman Old Style
Designed by Chris Fenwick
Cover by Chris Fenwick
Edited by Chris Fenwick

Continue the Enlightenment!

To those who fight for

universal single payer healthcare

for all Americans.

Mom's so sad. I wish she had just dropped me off here and left me here alone.

It's so awful to see her like this. She's still hoping for good news: some simple explanation. Well, Mom, it is a simple explanation. The bad cells are back and this time they're here for good.

Mom thinks – no, mom says she thinks – it's just a cold. Maybe the flu gave me this fever and that would explain my skin looking bad. I just have the flu. Maybe if I was Mom, I'd guess that too. I'd hang onto that notion. But she's not inside here with me. She never felt the bad cells when I had them last time. It's too bad she can't feel them because she's in pain anyway without knowing the difference. She suffers but she doesn't know what those bad guys feel like. So, she blames the fever on a flu bug. Not this time, Mom.

See, every other time I've gotten a fever since that doctor from Boston told her I was in remission, Mom freaked. She'd worry about the worst but didn't admit that this was what she was thinking. So, she just acted crazy. I guess I hate that the most. The way she tries not to look like she's afraid. Like she's the only one thinking the worst. Like every cold doesn't make me wonder if some of the bad cells came back. But I should've known all those other times it was nothing – that it didn't feel like bad cells, just sick cells. Well, I know now. Those colds weren't relapses. 'Cause they didn't feel like this.

It's too bad we spent so much time worrying before. Yeah, all that time she thought about me dying she could've relaxed. She didn't have to worry but she worried anyway. But then, so did I. Ever since I was seven, I've thought about dying. I didn't worry about being dead when I was a little kid. I didn't know any better. I just worried about Mom being sad.

But really, since then I've grown up a lot! How in the world could my mom believe that all this time I've been in remission – if she didn't mention it – I'd forget about cancer? Hospitals? Dying?

How can she seriously think that if she doesn't talk about the bad cells when I get a fever, I won't think of them on my own? If I was in remission for thirty years, I think I'd still believe that at any minute those bad cells would come back and that I'd finally lose, and they'd finally win.

Oh God, Mom's doing that really fast talk to total strangers thing again. It's not her fault. I know she's nervous. But now everyone in the waiting room knows she's flipping out too. Mom, do you honestly think the lady next to you is wearing a ball cap because she likes the Yankees? And the kid without eyebrows, who's he kidding?

Mom, relax, you're in a room filled with people who can't stop thinking about dying. They know you're whacked, they get it. But they got troubles of their own and on top of their own gunk, you're probably driving them crazy.

She's driving me crazy. I hate saying that because I love her so much.

Sometimes I wish she'd never had me. Not because I've had to fight these cells that want to kill me. Not even because I get scared that the bad cells will win. But because she's so scared. Because she's lived with my cancer almost more than I have, because she's so afraid I'll die. If I'd never been born, she'd never have had to worry about me dying. Maybe she and dad would have stayed together. Had a different kid. Me even, but with different cells. Yeah, that would have been great. If I'd only been born a few years later or earlier with good cells that weren't so yummy looking to all those bad ones.

Oh, thank god! They've called her up to the kiosk. She'll have somebody to talk really fast to that is paid to listen to her. What a weird job, being paid to listen to people so sick that it makes them crazy. Or people like my mom: people who love somebody so much that they go crazy watching them be sick. Sometimes I imagine the tables turned. Mom's gone through all this and I'm healthy. And I can't stand it. It's better this way, even if she is driving me crazy.

I have a teacher at school. Mrs. Welch. Mrs. Welch is the only person I've told about Mom and the scaredy-cat days we have at my house. Mrs. Welch gave me you, yeah you, my "magic" diary. She says it does magic because I can write in it really fast, just like Mom talks really fast, but nobody will hear me. They might look at me funny as I race through page after page of writing, but if those bad cells are back, they're going to look at me funny anyway.

Mrs. Welch says the diary's magic because time will go more quickly when I write in it. She says if I write every time I get upset, I'll look up and a whole lot of time will have gone by. She says if I write what I think about my mom in it: then I might understand her better too. Understanding my mom would be magic.

I like the idea of a diary. ("Journal" Mrs. Welch calls it because she's afraid I'll think she's treating me like a baby to call it a diary – you know fill it up with pages that start "Dear Diary" but I won't. I just think magic diary sounds better than magic journal, more poetic). And if this was just the flu, I was planning to grow up and be a famous writer some day. Some famous writer! What happened did I fall in love with the parenthesis and quotation marks all of a sudden? I read a book once that said only college kids use semi-colons 'cause it makes them look smart. Semi-colon, hmm, has a whole different meaning in this cancer unit. Don't think I'll use one of them either.

Anyway, I know the diary isn't magic. But I'll go along with Mrs. Welch on this one. 'Cause when I'm a famous writer, I'll write nothing but fantasy. One of my biggest fantasies is that everyone will want to read my diary from when I was just a kid trying to figure out life. Trying to figure out death – but none of my English teachers ever talks that way. Probably because these adults don't like thinking that way.

Still, I'm going to write fantasy stories about beautiful places and fairies and warlocks and magic wands that fix hurt feelings and make every angry person giggle right in the middle of saying something mean so nobody takes them seriously. Magic wands that can make your pimples go away because in the places I invent nobody will have anything worse than greasy hair or pimples! My fantasy lands won't have cancer treatment rooms or plastic pipelines put into little kid's hearts that feed them poison medicines that will *definitely* make them throw up but *might* also save their lives.

No, my stories will be about perfect places and perfect

smiles and perfect dragons who capture perfect little girls and then play Yahtzee with them until their mom comes home from work. Moms that never cry. Moms that don't smile at you with lips like sugar candy while they stare at you with eyes like broken hearts.

That's what my mom looks at me like. Sometimes her eyes are so red from crying and dark from no sleep: she looks like she has broken hearts where her eyes should be. Sometimes my wild imagination – that's what my dad says I have when I tell him about the stories, I'll write one day – sometimes my wild imagination almost lets me see real little broken hearts right in her pupils. I'd tell her they're there, but I think she already knows. And if she thought I could see them, those hearts would break wide open and so many tears would spill out that I just couldn't take it. So, we both keep quiet – with each other anyway – about what we already know.

She keeps quiet about me dying and I keep quiet about her crying. Hey, maybe I won't write fantasy stories after all. Maybe I'll write country music. "She keeps quiet 'bout me dyin' and I keep quiet 'bout her cryin'" – I'd have to write though because those country singers don't waste a lot of time in a song by singing the whole word.

I like this magic diary.

I looked up at the clock and 35 minutes have gone by. When doctors say they'll squeeze you in, I think they mean tack you onto the end.

Let's see now – what else should I write about?

Notopic deserves a fresh page, I think.

Let's see, maybe I should catch this MD up on my mom and dad and how all that happened. Hey MD. That's a great nickname for my magic diary. I can put MD on the cover and folks will think it belongs to a doctor and then they'll be afraid to touch it. It'll also explain the bad handwriting if anyone looks inside.

"We have proof, your honor, this can't possibly belong to a ninth-grade girl. Ninth grade girls have lovely penmanship! No, your honor, this messy thing must belong to a practitioner of the medical arts."

Plus, if folks see something they think belongs to a doctor, they'll just leave it alone. They'll just walk away from all the headaches that come from messing with a notebook the doctor needs.

Especially Dr. Borlasa. Nobody messes with her. She's my favorite. But maybe I'll talk about her again if I run into her again. In the meantime...

Where do I start?

I guess they used to be in love. I really don't remember it. I kind of don't believe it either. I mean I can understand loving each of them. I just can't see how they could have loved each other. My mom cries about stuff. Some of the stuff anybody would cry over. My dad never cries – not that I know about anyway – but he used to yell at my mom for crying.

My dad is smart and good at some things. But he's way too bad at other things. Mom says he's never been any good under pressure. My Nana agrees. Nana looks at me with this super intense look on her face and says, and I mean she says it all the time, "Your father is just NO GOOD in a crisis." And Nana doesn't mean "Sorry Mr. you got a sick kid" kinds of crisis. No, she means just about any little old crisis.

My Nana told me that one time the pipes froze in the basement where the water comes into the house from outside. Dad started fuming and cursing and went downstairs to fix the problem himself. Dad is a tax attorney, but he thinks plumbers are too expensive. Nana says plumbers shouldn't do their own taxes, and my dad shouldn't do his own plumbing. The way Nana tells the story it was quite a mess: water, tools, soaking wet rags and boxes strewn all over the basement floor. The boxes stored my dad's old books and stuff. All the while just more and more water pouring in.

Mind you, all my life, I've stayed with Nana when the folks weren't around. When I was little, and my mom had to work I was there almost every day. She lived right around the corner from us and Mom said we lived within 'spoiling distance.'

Not that Nana spoiled me, but I spoiled her.

Mom says I gave my Nana undivided attention, and then Nana would get out of control. I always thought it was funny that Mom thought my Nana couldn't control herself around me. She'd say, "Ma, quit telling Genevieve all those grown up stories. She doesn't need to know that stuff." But my Nana would just go right on telling me. She said she was an old lady and didn't know how long she'd be around and if she didn't tell me the stories, I might never learn them and that'd be a shame. So, she told me about her brothers and sisters and her parents and her school and about my father. Boy, Mom would get steamed. But I think Nana was right. I need to know what my family is really like.

So, Nana told me about this one-time Dad went downstairs with Mom's blow drier and thaw the pipes himself. I'm no plumber either so I don't know what went wrong, but once Dad was ankle deep in icy cold water, I guess he called for help. And Nana said the evening ended up being super expensive, especially because about the time the plumber was coming in the front door, dad was headed out the back door to "relax a little and get away from the mess." He got home about three a.m. The plumber had fixed the pipes. The basement had only an inch of water left in it. I was sound asleep in my crib. And Dad was "three sheets to the wind."

Of course, when Nana first told me that story, I never knew what she meant by "three sheets to the wind." One day, after Mom and Dad split, I asked mom to tell me her version of the frozen pipe story. It was all pretty much the same. Dad had ranted and raved. Dad had tried to fix them himself. Dad failed. Dad got mad. Dad got drunk. Mom said drinking was his way of coping. She told me that some people take medicine prescribed by a doctor. Some people find other ways to drug themselves. Bourbon was Dad's drug.

It's too bad in some ways that Mom thought I had to wait to hear stories like that 'cause by the time mom believed I was old enough to hear the frozen pipe story – or any of the others for that matter – it didn't matter. By the time I was about ten, I was well acquainted with my dad's routine. I could tell when he was mad. I could tell when he left, he'd be gone a while. And, I could tell when he was drunk.

Some people leave under certain circumstances enough times that after a while, you stop trying to make them stay. You get relieved they are gone, and you hope they don't come back. I love my dad, but I'm glad we don't live with him. His little routines are somebody else's problems now. Mom and me, we got our own stuff to deal with.

Don't get me wrong, MD. I'd be happy if my dad got over all this. I'd be happy if he learned that one way or another, we've got a finite amount of time together: even if I live to be 70. But what difference does it make if he only gets mad and storms off? I'd like to have him around someday, but I don't want him around until he learns to enjoy being with us. Nana says it'll never happen. Mom tells Nana to be quiet.

Three or four times I've wanted to ask my father why he didn't see a doctor and talk about what's bugging him or at least get medicine that wouldn't rot his liver. Nana says drinking all that bourbon will rot his liver. My liver's been compromised with chemotherapy. Why would anyone take chances like that? Anyway, I've always chickened out. I love my dad. But let's face it. Poor guy couldn't deal with a leaky pipe. He couldn't hold it together under mild circumstances. And that was before I got sick.

My dad's reaction to excess pressure was just to come unglued and then wander down to the Waverly tavern to re-cement his innards and be whole again for a few days. Like a glued together broken jar, my dad's twice as breakable the next time around.

Oh wait. Mom wants me to come up to the desk. Aw jeeze she looks awful. How can such a pretty woman look so bent in two? Stop gritting your teeth Mom, I'm coming.

Where'd they get that girl?

Hasn't she ever taken blood before? I remember being a little kid and wanting to become a doctor or a nurse, but I never wanted to be a phlebotomist. And not just because I couldn't say it for the first few years, I knew they existed. It's not that their jobs aren't just as important and all, but they never have an upside to the patient. It's never, "I came to bring you flowers," like the pink ladies from downstairs. Or, "Here are some new cards that came today." No, it's always just, "Hey gotta take blood!" A yick and a stick!

Some of them aren't so bad at what they do, but some of them must've gotten the job because they flunked sewing class or something and still wanted to use needles. Or maybe as kids they had voodoo dolls.

I wonder. When they stick their pins in me, does some little doll someplace start to cry?

Maybe I'm just grumpy. I keep waiting for the day when needle sticks are a thing of the past. And the day never seems to come.

Nana'd say, "Don't wish your life away." Funny that my Nana never changed her little sayings even when she would talk to me. Other people would look at her like, "Hey don't say those things to her. Don't you know your granddaughter could die!?! How can you say stuff like that?" I think maybe Nana knew what I knew. Just because somebody's told me I could die in a few months doesn't mean I'm necessarily any closer to dying than anybody else. Everyone's a fool to wish their life away: whether they think they have four months or four years or four decades.

I liked that Nana treated me like I was living instead of like I was dying. I never stopped hoping she was right. I guess I never will quit hoping.

Anyway, Mom told the phlebotomist lady we'd wait for the results. Man, she must be coming unglued. In the old days when we needed a checkup, she'd take me shopping or to lunch – now she doesn't want to leave the building.

Writing in this diary makes me think about how I think. I guess there's more magic in it than just making time go by. It makes me see my thoughts. I just wrote, "When we needed a checkup." When what I should have written was, "When I needed a checkup." But it has felt that every pain and bad cell and awful moment I have had, my mom has had with me.

Gee, if my dad couldn't hold up under pressure, it's sure the exact opposite of my mom. Sure, she cries and stuff – but I think that's just the way she releases the pressure – you know, so it doesn't make her explode. She's still here right by my side. I know she hates to cry in front of me, so she tries to hide it. Waits until she's convinced I'm asleep. She lets go of some of the stress and then she braces herself and takes more. My Poor Mom. I love you Mom.

Aw heck, us staying to hear the results means she thinks they will admit me. Who'll stay with me if she has to run home for my clothes and my Kazzu? Oh yeah, my Kazzu. I haven't told you about that yet, have I MD? Well I will tell you all about her when Mom runs to get her.

Because, oh great and powerful magic diary, it looks like from now on you'll be the one staying with me while Mom's gone.

Son of a gun, they want us at the desk again. At this rate, I'll never finish my story about my parents, their divorce, and the lady at the Waverly.

I better get mom to bring back my pencil box too, with all the stories I have to tell, I don't know how long this pen will last.

Mom's on her way to the house. It's official. I'm sick again. I wish they had let me go with her to the house. I don't think it's an any better thing that Mom's alone than it is that I'm alone. And she has to drive. Nana always told her she was the worst driver in the world without help. Worrying about a relapse of ALL – Acute Lymphoblastic leukemia – is definitely not help!

"Gee, Mrs. Flynn, ALL doesn't have to be a death sentence, but it is the way you drive!"

Now where was I before that nasty doctor interrupted my writing with his stupid decision to admit me? Oh yeah, Back to the story of my folks.

So, if bad plumbing could send Dad off for a night on the town: you can imagine what a kid with leukemia did for him. I remember that day that Mom and Dad came back into the emergency room where I waited with Nana. They came to get me. All the tests had come back from the doctor, and they were transporting me for the first time to the eighth floor. I was only seven, but I remember them sitting down and telling me I would need to, "Spend a lot of time at the hospital for a while." I remember Mom kept having to wipe her cheek. And I remember Dad. Dad kept telling her to. "Knock it off before you scare the kid to death."

Mom just wasn't tough enough in his opinion. But he's gone and she's still here. Seems pretty tough to me.

Did you ever see those movies where the guy is running along, and the bad guys shoot him in the leg? The bullet hits him in the upper thigh and then boom, down he goes. And he tears a piece of his sleeve off and ties it around his leg. Then, because he's the hero, he gets up and keeps running. HE RUNS ON A BROKEN LEG! Well that's what I think of with my mom, here.

She loves with a broken heart. It's gotta hurt like holy heck but she wraps it up and keeps loving.

My dad took the broken heart as a permanent injury. No more scenes, out for the rest of the movie!

I don't think my dad's a wimp or anything. In fact, I think he's average. My mom's spectacular in her ability to go on. My dad's just ordinary. Not deficient, just... What did Nana always call him? Just "run of the mill." How many people could run on a broken leg? And how many could love with a broken heart? Not too many I don't think – and anyway, he sure didn't sign up for those long nights on the eighth floor. I'm sure he thought marriage and having a kid would be more like his accounting job. Not an action movie with bullets, umm diseases, flying around everywhere. One violent scene followed by ten tragic ones.

Like the checkerboard dinners – he hated those scenes the most. Those checkerboard dinners – once those began – that was the beginning of the end. It was the second checkerboard dinner, the one put on by the other ladies at the bank where Aunt Pam worked that sent Dad away for two days.

And when he came back, he was so drunk he slept in the garage at the foot of the stairs. Maybe his legs were broken too. Shot through the thigh, but not the **kind of** character that gets up and keeps running. Or maybe his broken heart gave out. Nana said his pride exploded. Checkerboard dinners are sure tough on the pride.

But MD, considering we're alone, let me explain how they work.

See, lots of folks want to help when they hear about your sick kid. They see her hair falling out at school and they watch her weight drop and drop. Then the steroids kick in and your poor little seven-year-old looks like a monster. Her whole body swells up and she looks like she's eats like a horse. She moves stiffly because her bones all hurt. The nice folks that work with your sister at the bank, they want to help with the doctors' bills because they noticed that you sold your car.

So, they get together and invite the whole town and charge five dollars at the door and have silent auctions of junk nobody wants and do raffles and things. Then they go up to you and say, "We love your sister, Pam, so much and we're all worried about your little girl and we hope this helps." Then they put $847.21 into your hand and you turn on your heel hand the money to your wife and go and get drunk.

That's how Nana said a man's pride gets crushed. Well-meaning people stick their noses in his business. He's desperate so he takes their help. Then the man can't walk up the stairs in the garage anymore. He sleeps on the concrete. His legs aren't broken. There aren't any bullet holes. It's just that his pride's been crushed. He can't stand upright anymore without his pride. Next thing you know, he's so icky smelling drunk that the only good news is that if his heart is broken, it doesn't matter anymore. See, MD, with all that booze in him, he can't feel his heart anymore.

That time he slept in the garage, that was the last time he went to one of the checkerboard dinners. Oh, the town had more. Churches near our house had more. They all laid out their best fresh pies and bread sticks on the tables covered with checkered tablecloths, but they never saw my dad again. Nana said it's one of the few things she never blamed Dad for. Not being able to sit there and face the fact that he couldn't take care of his sick little girl without help from charity.

Nana said on that one she gave him, "a pass." Nana would say, "What kind of a society made a man beg others to save his kid's life?"

Mom and I still went to them. Nana went whenever she could.

Anyway, sometimes I liked the dinners. Heck, MD, I never understood about the money. So, I never had to care about my pride. And even though sometimes I couldn't stand the sad way everyone looked at me – people looked at me like that all the time. When I think back about it, the ones that went to those dinners didn't look at me with as much pity or pity me as often because they were on their best behavior. Nana said strangers were prepared to act like the checkerboard dinners were normal things in a way that Dad couldn't. Nana said strangers could go home and forget about the sick kid and the hospital bills, but my dad couldn't.

See, when people ran into me out of the clear blue, and I had a mask on to keep from catching some airborne illness, and a neckerchief tied onto my little bald head, that's when they looked at me with serious pity. Or maybe even disgust. Some people looked away from me as fast as if they had never seen me.

That was fine with me. "Nothing here to see folks. Move along." People got away with their discomfort. They could stare or freak. It was OK. Except for when Nana was around. Then. Well. Not so much.

Folks who freaked at the way I looked when Nana was around? Well, MD, let's say, they'd learn a thing or two. If Nana was with me when we ran into the pity people, she'd take the opportunity to fix their little wagon, too. See, everyday folks might not know about kids with cancer, but Nana would teach them. Nana took special care to teach the ones who looked disgusted. She'd always say, "I'll teach them a thing or two" or "I'm gonna fix their little wagon."

One day I heard a couple at the grocery store talk about me when Mom was talking to the nice guy at the deli. She was ordering organic lunchmeat or some other thing that took forever. She was always reminding the nice guy she didn't want any of those chemical additives. "There were too many chemicals in our lives already," she'd say.

But this one time I overheard an impatient woman in line behind us say to the man standing beside her, "Does that stupid woman think her kid's cancer is contagious? Of course, she doesn't. It's shameful. She must have her in that ridiculous mask for sympathy." They didn't know Nana was with us in the store. She had gone to get a jar of mustard (mom loves mustard on her ham sandwiches), and Nana had come up from behind them.

Well, MD, they learned a thing or two about cancer that day.

Nana plunked the mustard in the shopping cart and straightened up to talk to them. I was glad that the mask covered my face when Nana did her, I'm-getting-as-tall-as-possible posture thing she always does when she's ready to tell someone off.

Nana said, "Well, I'm sure I don't have to tell a couple of unwashed people like yourselves how many germs you have flying out of your mouth when you talk about things you know nothing about." Nana's face was flushing. Nana got rosy from eyebrows to neckline when she fixed peoples' wagons. "I'm sure you understand that a little child receiving chemotherapy has a compromised immune system! You know what that means? Of course, you do. That means she can catch whatever disgusting condition you two geniuses have."

Nana's face was now turning bright red, I mean like candy apple red, but the couple's faces were redder.

"My granddaughter gets lonesome at home and wants to come out into this filthy world and..." Now she was getting loud. As if her tone was increasing to match her flush. Both mom and the nice deli man had stopped taking and stared at her, "And well, for the life of me I don't understand why she'd want to be around filthy ignorant people like you. But somehow she does."

Mom covered her own mouth almost like she was somehow covering up Nana's. I think she would have, if she could have reached her. But no such magic, MD.

Nana went on, "I hope you never learn what it's like to have an illness so severe that some foul human being could pass on a cold or flu that could kill you. I hope you stay numb as a pounded thumb – with one exception!" And here was the point Nana really wanted to make, "I hope you at least learn to shut your mouth in public and keep your foul afflictions to yourself."

Mom started to cry.

The nice deli man reached over the case and put his hand on her shoulder. I could see his eyes welling with tears too.

Nana grabbed the back of my wheelchair and shoved me toward the frozen food isle. "C'mon Genevieve, let's go to a part of this store where I can cool off. And you can pick out a few different flavored popsicles for those lesions in your mouth that are always so sore."

Oh yeah, she fumed big time.

But that stuff never happened at the checkerboard dinners.

To tell you the truth, when I was this-kid-might-die sick, those dinners were the only places I could go in public and people wouldn't stare at my bald head or my swollen face. People who went to those checkerboard dinners knew what they were in for before they got there, and they weren't so surprised to see me.

Besides, the people were nice and there'd be music and food and kids from my school would go. We'd have fun. Too bad the doctors hadn't given my Dad the bill before they started the cancer treatments for me. Maybe he'd have realized we couldn't afford it right from the beginning. Maybe he could have just left us before he got his pride crushed. Before he found himself sleeping on the garage floor.

Maybe if he could have avoided the damage it did to his pride and if he could just have kept his self-esteem, maybe he could have handled the rest of the pressure the leukemia caused.

But I think those checkerboard dinners did so much **harm** he had to go away. Go away to a place where it wasn't so much work to be alive.

For some people it might not be so much work. Living, I mean. But for others it's 24/7. The lucky ones, the healthy folks: they have no idea how much work it is to be sick or to have a sick somebody you love. I think **some** folks think being sick just looks boring or dull. It's anything but: because it's so much work.

Sometimes people look off into space and that makes them look bored. They aren't bored – they're weary. It isn't boring and it isn't dull. It's exhausting. And it isn't just exhausting, it's **exhaustingly** frustrating.

It's frustrating when no one answers your questions. It's beyond frustrating when no one knows the answers to begin with. But it's maybe most frustrating when you know the answers and you think you are following the rules they give you and you still don't know if they'll work. Sometimes you can't be sure the answers will be answers at all.

Some parents even fool their kids. I've had friends on the eighth floor who say their parents fall asleep or watch TV while they are throwing up or bleeding or crying. I can't believe it. I believe they try to watch TV. Make it look like they are watching. But inside they're like the rest of us, kids included, who just want to get it over with. All the while, trying not to say the wrong thing. Trying to act normal. Trying to spend their time next to YOUR bed. Holding YOUR hand. Keeping YOU safe. Without losing THEIR minds.

It's a lot of work to sit next to me when poison's dripping into my veins and not go batty. (My teacher calls crazy people batty. I think it's funny. I see a bat every time she says it. When I write my first fairy tale novel, I'm going to have a little bat in it who is pretty and has lots of earrings to call attention to her highly-effective ears and has black lacey wings and flits around scary places cheering people up and I will call her Batty-Patty).

Anyway... I don't think some people can stand all the work it is to stay sane up on the eighth floor. Not going batty with their dying relatives fading before them. Not puking at the bad smells. Not fainting at the sight of great big medicine tubes hooked into the little tiny kids.

If they aren't lucky enough to have an imagination that takes them other places inside their heads, then they have to go places in real life. Places where it's less work to be a person with a broken heart or crushed pride or both.

I think it must be a lot less work to go to the office or to the little restaurant near our house or to the waitress's apartment: the one that works at the little restaurant. It must be. Because my dad went to all three of those places while mom and I sat on the eighth floor. While I was picturing BattyPatty hovering around Mom and who knows what Mom was picturing.

Mom says she doesn't blame Casey. That's the waitress's name. Mom says Casey thought she was helping dad. Casey was just trying to help Dad cope with everything he had to deal with. Nana yelled at Mom one time and they both started crying. She yelled at her something about "While Casey was helping Dad to recover from Genevieve's cancer, did she ever wonder who would help you recover from Casey?"

Nana loves my mom, but I think she hurt her that day. She hurt her by not pretending that everything abnormal was normal. I think mom copes by acting like we're supposed to be living through all of this. Mom pretends that everything awful is supposed to be happening and we are supposed to get used to it. That's why I have BattyPatty hanging around her. I wish Mom could see her there. Maybe she'd feel a little safer.

I think Mom was just too batty when she learned about Casey to handle anything more. So, she acted like Casey was supposed to be there for Dad.

Whoa! Good one BattyPatty!

Last year I overheard Mom tell my aunt Jane about the old days when Dad was with Casey and I was a hairless chemo-kid. Aunt Jane was on the phone and mom said, "If you can't find someone to blame for something as cruel as your kid's cancer, how can you find someone to blame for anything as stupid and unimportant as a husband sleeping around?" Mom went on acting chill and unaffected, "At least Genevieve has a disease the doctors can cure. William has a condition that has cost him my love and respect."

She sounded so grown up all the time when I was in remission. I guess her attitude came from the opposite of what she told Aunt Jane. When someone gives you back something as valuable as your kid's life, who cares if they ever give you back your husband? In a fair trade: Mom felt like she had gotten the thing she wanted most and lost the thing she relied on least.

But back when I was a kid. Back when I still had the cancer. She never sounded so peaceful about it all. Nope, she sure sounded angry. I hate that sound. That angry sound a mom makes when it's actually anger made of fear. When she was talking fast in the waiting room earlier today, I thought for a minute I heard that sound come back.

MD, I sure hope my mom never gets so scared again that she gets mad like that. It makes me feel like I'm a little kid again. A sick little kid.

Anyway, Dad didn't come back home after mom found out about Casey. And that was just as well. Mom might not have blamed Casey but I'm pretty sure she blamed Dad. I don't have to tell you, so did Nana.

I guess now, while I'm thinking about it, so do I. What kind of a dumb man finds checkerboard dinners so awful that he'd hurt his wife that bad? Not just any wife? My Mom! The mom of a sick little kid.

Hey, MD, all this writing and remembering is making me so tired. I can't keep my eyes open. Another magic thing – I'm falling asleep in a hospital bed all by myself. Who knew I could be that brave? In my first fairy tale, I'll have a magic book that kids read and get brave. Zzzzzzzzzzzzzzzzzzzzz

Sweet dreams MD.

I woke up and Mom was back.

The room was all dark, but I could see her in the recliner chair on the left-hand side of my bed. I could feel her too. She wasn't quite holding my hand. She had her hand, palm up, lying on the bed and she had my hand, palm down, resting on it. That's how you hold a hand with an IV in it. You cradle it in yours, so you don't bend it and hurt the little vein with the needle in it. Moms of kids with cancer know exactly how to hold the IV hand.

The room was pitch dark, but I could see she had brought a number of things back for me from home. Setting on top of the little bureau across from the foot of my bed was a stack of my schoolbooks. I can't see it for sure, but I'll bet tomorrow's hospital issue apple sauce that my backpack's on the floor over there too. She must've emptied the books out of it so she could put my clothes in it. So, Mom stopped by the house for clothes and then went to the school to get me some homework.

I guess Mom thinks I'll be here a while.

She grabbed my school stuff and then what? She must've lugged all my textbooks under her arm if she used my backpack for clothes. I'm sure that must be what happened. I haven't got any other suitcase. Not yet, anyway. I'm guessing this because that little Barbie suitcase I took to the hospital for treatments when I was seven just wouldn't work. Mom loves me and my teen-aged pride too much to show up here with the Barbie suitcase.

Or she still just hates the suitcase.

I remember one time after I went into remission, I got invited to Jill Wentworth's house for a sleep over party. I packed up the Barbie travel bag and brought it down the stairs. Mom cried. I went right back upstairs, and I never took it out from under my bed again.

From then on out, for sleep overs, I packed an extra pillowcase. All the kids thought I rocked 'cause my mom let me drag a pillowcase around town. My poor mom, cool was her consolation prize for heartbroken. Moms of sick kids are the most creative of all. What is it that Mr. Dunsten always says? "Necessity is the mother of invention." He says it when he's talking about finding a way to do homework in a cafeteria full of screaming kids. He ought to see what kind of inventions "necessity mothers" when a mom and a sick kid are trying to forget about cancer!

Maybe we'll go luggage shopping when I get out of the hospital. I enjoy going to Freeport. My favorite restaurant is down there, and Mom loves the trout pond in the middle of the big sporting goods store. Or maybe we'll just get their catalogue and see what they have for big girls to tote things around in. And they'll put your name on it too.

That place has everything. I wonder if they have a special line of luggage just for taking junk to the hospital.

And today's LL Bean remission line of luggage features this lovely pink and purple tote bag. You can have it monogrammed so the other little bald kids don't inadvertently grab the bag with the wrong wigs in it.

Hey if you're going on a remission trip, does that make you a remissionary? See what I did there, MD? (never mind)

Anyway, so LL Bean always makes specialty stuff. They could make remissionary bags with a place for schoolbooks and a place for a toothbrush: right next to the barf bag. Oh yeah, they'll need a barf compartment. No cancer kid can get by without a place to puke. I remember the car always had a barf basin in the front seat and one in the back seat. Aw nuts, back to barfing in the car again.

I don't know if I can do all this all over again. Man, I don't want to think about that now.

OK, Genevieve, finish designing the LL Bean bag. School book compartment. Toothbrush holder. Barf bag. Don't need shampoo compartments or hairbrush hide-aways. But there'll be this lovely pop up wig stand! It needs an address book and stationery and pens. And I guess a secret compartment to hide your diary. I won't be traveling without my magic diary.

Oops, Mom stirred a little. She can't sleep much in here. She might close her eyes, but she's always half awake. Her feet are shifting under the white cotton blanket she has covering her from neck to toe. I bet some nice nurse put it on her. It looks like the ones they make the beds with. It's not real warm, but it seems to be doing the trick. She's sleeping at least.

Closer to me than the bureau is the hospital tray table. That's where the folks from dietary services put your tray of food. It's where they leave the remote control if you can afford to rent the TV service from the hospital and it's where they stack cards or place flowers when someone sends you them so you can get a look at everything without pulling on a cord or a tube or a wire that's sticking in you somewhere. Once you're all hooked up to the medicines and monitors, you don't want to pull on anything you aren't supposed to pull.

Unless you're lonely. Because when those wires get yanked, someone always comes in to make sure you're OK. Sometimes I wonder if they know that you know pulling on a cord will make them come in to see you. They must. They're busy and they don't stay so long, but they're always nice about it.

The people who work here leave notes and flowers on the tray table for a little while. Then when the nurses come in to check on you, they move the stuff to the windowsill or over to a shelf. After that you can only see them from far away. But that's OK; once you've seen them you needn't stare at them to remember what they're about.

"Get well soon." "You and your mom take care."

People who write to a sick kid don't know what to write, so they avoid all the reality and make small talk. Well-wishers get guilt crushed when they realize what they're thinking. They never write what's nagging at them. How many ways can you write, "Gee, it's awful you're going through that! Glad it's not me!"

Of course, no one would ever write that. But it would be OK. I'm glad it's not them too.

Anyway, I like it when the nurses hang my cards up on the cork board across the room. It makes the wall look brighter.

The room I'm in this time is made for two people. There's a bed on the right but there's nobody in it. I love an empty bed in my room. And it's not because I don't want a roommate. It's because an empty bed means one less kid with cancer.

Or maybe, one less kid without cancer too.

Not everyone who comes to a kids' ward in a hospital is a cancer patient. Sometimes the kids got injured. Or worse. Sometimes kids got injured on purpose! One time a kid was in the other bed and the police came and pulled his dad right out of the chair next to him. It shocked me. Then it scared me. It all happened so fast. There was a lot of shouting and yelling things the little boy shouldn't have heard. I hadn't invented BattyPatty yet, so I didn't know how to stop him – or me – from bursting into tears. The dad kept saying he was sorry. The mom was crying and yelling at the cops.

Funny thing about most grown-ups with a kid in the hospital. They must always think the kid in the next bed is deaf. Yeah, they sure can say things that little kids shouldn't ever hear. I've heard a lot of things I shouldn't ever have heard.

Back when my dad came to the hospital, he said stuff he should never have said. Other adults and plenty of little kids heard him. I heard him too, when he thought I was asleep. But I wasn't.

Sometimes Dad spouted off when he was – what's Nana's word? – plastered. Then he'd just talk about stuff I didn't want him to tell me. Sometimes he'd tell me way more than I wanted to know about him and Mom. I wanted to yell at him. Dad! Quit with the overshare! Will ya? PUHLEASE! Well I didn't know overshare then as a term. But I sure know now that that's what he was doing.

Other times he'd just tell me how this wasn't his fault and he'd tell me to stop looking at him, "like that." What did I know about looking at him? I was a little kid. Nana says his guilt was all "transference." I guess she meant that he took the guilt he should've been feeling about some of the stuff he did and shifted it over onto the fact that he had a sick kid, and he couldn't do anything about it.

Well, I couldn't do anything about it either, Dad. Maybe that's what my face was saying when I looked at you that way you didn't like.

Nana said he'd pick on me because he felt like a failure.

And then, one day, he stopped coming back. So, maybe he was right.

When my dad stopped visiting it was fine by me. Some poor kid with tonsillitis didn't need to know that the cancer girl's dad liked to prescribe his own medicine. Kids who weren't so sick could learn a lot sleeping in a bed next to a kid who was pretty bad off.

It was surprising to some of my mom's friends that visited me that there'd be a kid with a broken leg or tonsillitis right in the next bed.

Of course, there's always a kid with tonsillitis or some basic, not-too-dangerous issue at the hospital. I call them the "one-timers." They come here once, but they're never coming back. And they and their parents know that they're never coming back. They're not mixed in with us might-die sick kids too often, but sometimes it can't be helped. The folks that run the hospital try to keep those healthy kids all together. In doing that, they have a better chance of keeping all us might-die kids together, too.

It makes sense. Some innocent young kid coming in here for a little procedure and seeing another kid all hooked to tubes or with a bag of blood and urine coming out from under the bed or missing clumps of hair or barfing all the time just scares the one-timers. It's no fun being scared. And them being scared doesn't do the rest of us any good. So, they're better off kept away.

I remember back the last time I was on the eighth floor. I was in a three-person room. The kid next to me had been in a fire or something. His back was burned, and he had all these skin grafts. I was just in for chemo and I had been getting it a while so most of the ugly side effects had already come and gone. If I'd had hair, I would have looked like any other kid. But this poor boy he looked like a special effect artist from one of those *Terminator* movies had gotten a hold of him. And his burns wouldn't stop – I don't know what the word would be – seeping. The nurses had put some kind of gauze on a lot of his back, and it had this yellow shiny stuff coming through it.

It looked like pure agony.

When someone moved his sheet and it tugged on one of those gauze strips, he'd let out a wail like nothing I'd ever heard. His reaction seemed worse than just a moan, or a cry. The element of surprise wasn't helping. Maybe it's because so many of the wounds were behind him and he couldn't see the pain coming. Hurting just snuck up on him in a real mean way that made him suffer with a surprise jolt. I think it tortured the person who'd been moving the sheet too. He or she almost always jumped when the boy cried out.

After a day or two of random torment, the nurses just left the sheet off him. He was naked except for the oozing dripping gauze stuck to his back and one of his legs. You could tell he didn't care. He was pretty doped up and besides, nobody was pulling on his bandages anymore.

Anyway, the boy and I were all alone one afternoon when this cute little girl came in. She had just had her appendix taken out. The floor must have been busy to have them put us all together like that. The little girl was OK. She was groggy from her operation though and didn't have a clue that we were there. After about an hour an older lady came in to see her. I think it must've been this girl's grandmother. She took one look at that burned boy laying between me and her granddaughter and she screamed.

Poor lady.

Her yell made me jump. The older lady looked over at me. She apologized. Then her eyes went back to the boy. She stared at him for about five minutes. Then she went over to the big curtain – the kind that has tracks in the ceiling so that doctors or nurses can make a little curtain room around your bed – you know a room with curtain walls, right in the middle of the bigger room you are all staying in. And she pulled the curtain around the boy's bed.

Then nobody could see him.

Not the grandma. Not her granddaughter when she woke up. Not me. Not anyone.

I held my breath and grabbed my IV pole. I crawled down the end of my bed. Then I could see her feet on the ground near her granddaughter's bed. Her feet were pointed away from me and away from the burned boy. Even though she pulled the curtain and didn't have to look at him: she still made sure she stood on the side of the bed that would keep her back to him. She didn't even want to stand facing his direction.

I don't think she wanted her mind to remember the boy was there.

Poor lady. She didn't know any better. A burned little boy is still a little boy.

The saddest part of all? The body that little lady can't stand to look at – well, he still has to look out at her from deep inside those burns.

I've seen some pretty scary messes that used to be normal looking little kids. I'll never look away. Never. Never. Maybe it's because I got used to seeing them when I was so little. They don't scare me like they do grown-ups. I was young when I first made friends with hurt kids and with sick kids. I was one of them. I had tubes hanging from my arms, my chest, and hair falling from my head. I'm glad the other kids don't shock and scare me the way grown-ups seem to get shocked and scared. These other little kids need me, I think.

If I don't look at them, who will?

Mrs. Welch says, "Your eyes are the windows to your soul." I try hard to look in their eyes. So, their souls can see me recognizing their existence. No matter how tortured a soul's body might look, I'm still not looking away.

Magic Diary, I'm tired. Do I really have to come back to all of this? Do I really have to watch my mom sleep in hospital rooms and hope for empty beds next to me?

The nurse is here. She's going to wake up Mom. She needs the IV hand. I love you Mom. I'm sorry she's waking you up.

"OK, here's your pencil box and here's that ragged old Kazzu." Then Mom repeated what she always says with a rehearsed air of disgust, "Genevieve, why don't you ever let me wash that thing?"

That's how I knew Mom was feeling a little better. Getting back to normal. She was back to harping on my lousy habit of dragging around a 13 ½ year old giraffe. Well, stuffed toy giraffe. Let's be quite certain that the hospital has rules against real giraffes.

Why wouldn't I let her wash it? Was she out of her mind? That long neck had about 4 more years left in it if I was super gentle. And that's with Nana sewing a scarf to it that "firmed it up a little bit." But, I'm sorry to say, Kazzu was never as cuddly after Nana performed the scarf surgery on her. I think she sewed a bunch of those red and white striped coffee stirrers into her neck – sort of like a brace – on the inside.

Yup, great thing about the hospital. The doctors and nurses work on fixing what ails their little patients while the grandmothers and moms wait for hours on end in the cafeteria. After a while, everything in that cafeteria becomes a tool for repair or distraction or both. Nana would say, "Your dad never comes to the cafeteria because they don't have HIS medicine here." Nope Nana, you're right. No bourbon in the beverage cart. And I don't have to tell you what Mom would say by now, do I MD? "Oh Ma. Be quiet."

And then Nana would wink at me and we'd both smile.

That old routine my Nana had: the one where she'd get my mom worked up enough to "shush" her always made the most awkward situation a little less tense and a little more like a comedy sketch. You know the ones, where the guys pull on each other's ears or nose. They'd make a funny noise and then all of them would laugh instead of cry. "Slapstick," that's what Nana called it.

Phil, my best friend on the street where we lived, he loved slapstick. He'd come to our house saying he was there to see me, but then Phil and Nana would sit on the couch and watch those old black and white shows and laugh and laugh. I'd roll my eyes at them and Nana would wink at me. That's how I learned early-on when she was just pulling a gag on my mom like those boys on the TV pulled the slapstick on each other. No matter what **anyone did** or said, it was never supposed to hurt. And you always knew for sure because it was all in Nana's wink.

Phil and I are still friends. We aren't in many of the same classes anymore because I was so sick for those two years. I never quite caught up to the kids in my class who never had leukemia. They still consider me a ninth grader at school. And if all goes well, I can graduate with Phil and the rest of my friends. But I take most of my classes in the eighth-grade units. The only classes I'm all caught up in are History and English Comprehension. Nana said it's because I read so well. Truth? There's not much else to do in a waiting room but read. Until now. Now I can top that. Now I can write too!

Anyway, Nana said after all the medical procedures I've lived through, they should just graduate me now and make me a doctor. Mom shushes her. Nana winks.

The nurse came into to check on my chemo drip and draw a little blood. Ha. A little blood. I wish they'd let BattyPatty just take the blood for them. At least she's magic. Oh, and imaginary.

Anyway. They're making sure the stuff that isn't sick yet, doesn't get sick because of the treatment. Trust me, MD, there's nothing worse than letting your calcium, potassium and those other *iums* get low and passing out or having a few convulsions. So yeah, I get it. It's kind of necessary.

Once the nurse had her necessities collected from me, mom lugged the schoolbooks over to my bed and handed me a note from Mrs. Welch. Mrs. Welch is my home room teacher and my English teacher. She talked to all the other teachers to get class assignments for me. I'll tape her note in here, MD, so I don't have to rewrite it.

Dear Genevieve,

How is your "magic" diary working? Have you started writing in it yet?

Everyone at school is sending you our best wishes that you get better: pronto! Each of your science and math textbooks have bookmarks in the chapters where you left off and, on those book-marks the instructions for the next week are written. Mr. Murray says to take your time on the math and go at your own pace. He said you're already way ahead of the rest of the class anyway. (Good job Genevieve!)

Mr. Dunsten and I have decided that as long as you do all your history reading assignments, we'll consider that your English comprehension work too. Remember, you won't be in his class for the lectures so make sure you get the full meaning out of your assignments! So, Mr. Dunsten and I will each evaluate your work for our respective classes. You need to be careful with your punctuation and spelling! It's your English composition grade too!

Mr. Dunsten said you 9th graders are just finishing up the unit on World War II. He tells me the war has ended in Europe. How wonderful. But now you've got to read the chapter about ending the war in the Pacific. That's a lot to digest so be sure and ask for help if you need it.

I hope to get in to visit you during my flex time this week. I'm shooting for Friday. Perhaps you will show me some of your journal by then. (Hint! Get writing!)

All my best,

Mrs. Welch

Wow. Won't she be surprised when she sees just how much I've used this diary! Mrs. Welch can be a funny teacher. Sometimes I think she knows that I'd at least try any lesson she assigned. Then other times, oh well, doesn't matter. She'll see how good her idea was when she gets here.

Hmmm. "Be sure and ask for help if you need it." I'd like to have her help me get out of these awful history reading assignments. MD, they are sooooo boring. Oops. My science teacher, Mrs. Dolan says boring makes holes, I need to say tedious. Well they are tedious. And I swear sometimes I feel like it makes holes in my head to read this stuff.

The worst thing of all for a little kid who is already battling cancer is that some of those WW II stories were giving me nightmares. Why do I need to read such sad stuff? I'll ask Mrs. Welch that question on Friday. Maybe I can put that assignment off for good. I'll see if Mom will let me not do the reading until after Mrs. Welch gets here on Friday. **Seriously!** I've had enough of gas chambers and death camps.

Nuts!

I asked Mom and she said, (MD pretend I'm using a prissy voice), "Seeing as it's your English and your history assignment I think you'd better get it done."

Ugh. OK, MD, Mom's off to the Cafeteria tool chest for a bite to eat and I think I'll tackle the reading and get it over with so I can move on to better things. Who ever thought Mr. Murray's pre-algebra problems would be better things?

I'll be back when the that history chapter's done.

Harry S Truman, I HATE YOU!

I hate you. I hate you. I hate you. How could you do anything so horrible? So disgusting? So despicable! You dropped not one nuclear bomb on people. You dropped two. TWO! One. Two. MD, sounds so simple. Easy counting. A two-year-old can count to two. But they didn't need a two-year-old to decide that one wasn't enough, did they Harry S Truman? No, you decided one wasn't enough. And so, you dropped another one. One plus one makes two. Mr. Murray wouldn't be very happy with my math skills if that's all I ever learned to do with them.

But wait, Mr. Murray, the bigger numbers come in handy here too. How about 580. Five-hundred and eighty meters above a hospital, that's where you decided the bomb should be exploded. Yes Mr. Murray, I remember that a meter is 3.28 feet. Mom left her iPad here. See I can figure this stuff out. So, I know Harry – I'm going to call you Hateful Harry – that you dropped a uranium bomb just 1,902.4 feet above a hospital. A HOSPITAL. Like the one I'm sitting in right now. It was the Shima Hospital. What if another man like you was alive today? A man with anger toward my government? A man who would drop a bomb above the Rosewood Medical Center and then just let horror rain down from the sky. Let it rain down on me?

No, Mr. Dunsten didn't assign all this reading from that little history book of ours. Our history book only devoted – let me count – 17 pages to the whole war in the pacific. And yes. I know they bombed us first and I know that they were bad to the people in concentration camps from China to the Philippines. But we're better than that! You were supposed to be better than that!

I got on the Internet. Mom doesn't always like me to look up random things on the internet, so she put web page blocks on her iPad. But the funny thing is, she never thought I'd look up words like "eyewitness account" and "effects of radiation poisoning." Nobody worries that their 14-year-old will go to the websites about U.S. wars. In fact, most parents would like it if we did, I think.

Not my mom, she doesn't think about that stuff, that's the

only reason she doesn't block it.

But those people who make the censorship programs. They are so worried we'll look at naked bodies, they couldn't care less if we look at dead ones. They should make an ad for this software, "Kill communities, don't expand them!" That's their motto. "We'll encourage your kids to be 'patriots.' Turn them on to history. Not sexuality. With the new Americans-Are-Afraid-of-all-the-Wrong-Things software, your kids will learn to fear each other and love war instead."

Nuts! I'm so angry. Look, Hateful Harry. I searched the web. I found all kinds of information about your bombs. I read that 80,000 people died in Hiroshima in the first 10 seconds! I learned that you blew 60,000 buildings to smithereens. Sixteen of those buildings were hospitals and 32 more were first aid clinics.

Hospitals.

I also found the writings of a Dr. Michihiko Hachiya. He's one of the 85 doctors that survived the bombing of Hiroshima. Sixty-five others were pulverized by you. I read part of his diary. This is what he wrote:

"It was all a nightmare — my wounds, the darkness, the road ahead.

My movements were ever so slow; only my mind was running at top speed.

Some [people] looked as if they had been frozen by death while in the full action of flight; others lay sprawled as though some giant had flung them to their death from a great height.

I saw nothing that wasn't burnt to a crisp. Streetcars were standing and inside were dozens of bodies, blackened beyond recognition. I saw fire reservoirs filled to the brim with dead bodies that looked as they had been boiled alive. In one reservoir I saw one man, horribly burned, crouching beside another man who was dead.

Others moved as though in pain, like scarecrows, their arms held out from their bodies with forearms and hands dangling. These people puzzled me until I suddenly realized that they had

been burned and they were holding their arms out to prevent
the painful friction of raw surfaces rubbing together."

Oh, Hateful Harry, I can't stop crying. Some giant **had** flung
them to their death. **You**. The United States. Scientists who
think dropping an atom bomb on people makes sense. Hateful
Harry, I have seen small amounts of the pain he describes. I
have seen the little boy nobody wants to look at because his
skin is burned off his back. I can almost feel the pain when
their arms touch their bodies as they walk. That's why they
moved the sheet off the little boy next to me.

Hateful Harry, how could you?

And then I read about the radiation poisoning. The vomiting. The hair falling out. I have vomited until I thought I would
die. I have lost all my hair. And now I have read about you
doing this to people who were healthy. They had no cancer. No
cancer but you. You were their cancer.

And Hateful Harry, I read websites that said Emperor Hirohito was ready to surrender. But before he could, you did it
again. This time you dropped a plutonium bomb on them. The
stories told on a website put up by the Atomic Heritage foun-
dation tell an even worse story with higher death tolls and
more devastation than the good Dr. Hachiya recounted. Why
did you drop a second one? A different one? Did you want to
see if every kind of bomb you had would work?

And then I read your words. The words you used when you
told my great grandparents about why it was okay to kill all
those people. I watched the newsreel as you explained – without expression – the cancer you gave to the Japanese people.

You said:

"WITH THIS BOMB, WE HAVE NOW ADDED A NEW AND
REVOLUTIONARY INCREASE IN DESTRUCTION TO SUPPLE-
MENT THE GROWING POWER OF OUR ARMED FORCES..."

You threatened, "EVEN MORE POWERFUL FORMS ARE IN
DEVELOPMENT. IT IS AN ATOMIC BOMB. IT IS A HARNESS-
ING OF THE BASIC POWER OF THE UNIVERSE. THE FORCE

FROM WHICH THE SUN DRAWS ITS POWER HAS BEEN LOOSED AGAINST THOSE WHO BROUGHT WAR TO THE FAR EAST."

Oh, Hateful Harry, how dare you compare yourself to the sun. Although, the sun causes cancer too.

Then you made a terrible promise, "WE ARE NOW PREPARED TO DESTROY MORE RAPIDLY AND COMPLETELY EVERY PRODUCTIVE ENTERPRISE THE JAPANESE HAVE IN ANY CITY. WE SHALL DESTROY THEIR DOCKS, THEIR FACTORIES, AND THEIR COMMUNICATIONS. LET THERE BE NO MISTAKE, WE SHALL COMPLETELY DESTROY JAPAN'S POWER TO MAKE WAR."

Because the Japanese leaders wouldn't stop fighting you said, "THEY MAY EXPECT A RAIN FROM THE AIR THE LIKE OF WHICH HAS NEVER BEEN SEEN ON THIS EARTH."

I guess you thought killing all those people would make sense. You hoped so. You didn't know. You treated it like a game of chance, "WE HAVE SPENT MORE THAN $2 BILLION ON THE GREATEST SCIENTIFIC GAMBLE IN HISTORY, AND WE HAVE WON, BUT THE GREATEST MARVEL IS NOT THE SIZE OF THE ENTERPRISE, ITS SECRECY, OR ITS COST, BUT THE ACHIEVEMENT OF SCIENTIFIC BRAINS IN MAKING IT WORK."

Scientific brains with no soul attached. Political brains with no heart attached.

And now Hateful Harry. You too are dead. But you got to live to be a nice old man. A nice old man that left us an uncertain future. You said, "BOTH SCIENCE AND INDUSTRY WORK TOGETHER UNDER THE DIRECTION OF THE UNITED STATES ARMY, WHICH ACHIEVED A UNIQUE SUCCESS IN AN AMAZINGLY SHORT TIME." And you called it "THE GREATEST ACHIEVEMENT OF ORGANIZED SCIENCE IN HISTORY."

No Hateful Harry. It is not. My chemotherapy is better. My Nana's blood pressure medicine is better. She's not here with me right now because she had a stroke. She's getting better and they have put her on a new medicine to stop her from having another stroke. And her medicine is a greater science achievement than your bomb dropped on her hospital would ever be.

What I don't get, and I will never get, is: How you could have bragged about what your science did? How in the world could you have bragged about your science in the face of all that misery?

How am I ever going to write about this chapter assignment for Mr. Dunsten tomorrow? I'll never get a good grade when he knows that I did my history homework. And I've seen kids with their skin burned away. And I hate Harry Truman.

D

ear Genevieve,

May I first beg your forgiveness for my actions on both August the 6th and August the 9th way back in 1945. I do not apologize because of the very passionate way you wrote of me here in your diary. I apologize as I have apologized to myself every day since that fateful time. While I was president, after I retired, and long after I died, I felt sadness about my actions. But unlike you, dear Genevieve, I have never questioned them.

I see you did more homework than your teacher had assigned. May I say how much I admire your initiative. I'm sure by digging further into the story, you learned more about me than you could glean from the newsreel after the 1st bombing. But, in case you did not, please let me tell you a little more.

I beg you to indulge me, Genevieve. It's not that I hope to make excuses for my actions. You are right when you infer that there is no excuse for ruthlessly killing tens of thousands of people. Did I know it would be rules? I suppose that I did. I must tell you now, my request to the bombardiers to minimize civilian casualties with the first bomb indicates how little I understood the hell we were unleashing. Looking back, my denial of the destructive power of our nuclear weapons seems naïve at best. But as you were right to point out in your commentary, I knew what horrors would unfold when I dropped the second one. Did you know that there were 14 bombs in the cue? I tell you now in complete honesty, I am forever grateful that the other 12 – no other nuclear devices since then – have been used in war.

So, while I offer no excuse, I do hope to explain the reasoning behind my decision to go ahead with the Manhattan Project, a program started my predecessor, Franklin D. Roosevelt. And no, Genevieve, this is not to shift blame from my own shoulders and onto his. It is, again, merely the course of events that led to my approval to drop the bombs.

As you noted the project cost nearly two billion dollars. Only 10 percent of that went into constructing the bombs themselves. The other 90 percent paid for the development of the technology and paid the salaries of almost 130,000 individuals who brought this deadly technology to its destructive fruition. The project was a shared arrangement with our allies, Great Britain and Canada. We might have had more allies in the project had not the axis powers in the late 1930s and early 1940s brought every other great power to its knees on one side of the world or another.

The only other power great enough to help build the ultimate weapon of war – which we thought would assure world peace – was the USSR. The United Soviet Socialist Republic no longer exists. Europe is a big place. The Soviet Union stretched from one side of that continent to the other. After decades of wars to keep either side of their reach from fraying, the Soviets eventually let go. The USSR splintered. You now call that country by many names. The largest off shoot is Russia.

We did not share our technology with the Soviets. Nor did we ask them for help. We feared the Soviets. In fact, we feared them so much that our desire to contain them played into my decision to detonate the atomic bombs over those two Japanese cities. We pinned our hopes on our new technology. If our nuclear weapons had not caused Emperor Hirohito to surrender, we had committed ourselves to invade Japan just three months later, in November. And we would not have invaded them alone. The Soviets had pledged to join us in what promised to be a very bloody ground war.

I have written of this many times. My memoirs are full of the explanations for my actions. The timeline, as the deadliest war in human history raged on, is available for you to read. But I do not want to just brush you off to do more research. When I became president, I knew less about the Manhattan Project than you learned in Mr. Dunstons' class. When I inherited the highest office in the nation, I had only my wits to save me. No political or military machine had groomed me for the job. If ever in history fate took hold, it did the day Franklin Delano Roosevelt died.

I was not Franklin's original vice president. Nor was I his second. Franklin served three terms, first with John Nance

Garner and then Henry A. Wallace as his second in command. When Franklin died just 82 days into his fourth term, I had been vice president for only those 82 days. I knew nothing of the Manhattan project. Furthermore, unbelievable now as it may seem, Secretary of War Henry L. Stimson did not brief me on the project for nearly two weeks: not until the 25th of April.

Stimson told me that a combination of efforts had engineered an uncertain yet likely and powerful way to end the years of fighting. Genevieve, did your history book tell you how many people had died in that war? I'm sure it told you of the six million Jews exterminated by Adolf Hitler and his Nazi regime. Millions more died on the battlefield. And countless millions died of the starvation and deprivation caused by war. But possibly the most chilling factor to me, when considering a ground war with Soviet assistance, was the 35 million Soviet peasants who died as a result of the way their government fought that war. Genevieve, in the years the second world war raged on, encompassing every inhabited continent of the earth – on average – 30,000 people died each and every day!

I join you in your outrage at the thought of 80,000 lives winking out in an instant. But I believed then and believe still – when I have nothing but time devoted to thought – that my dreadful decision saved lives. In 1963 I wrote a letter to Irv Kupcinet of the *Chicago Sun Times* and back then I guessed that my decision saved a million lives. I can no longer second guess that number.

I am more haunted by one other consequence of creating those atomic weapons. It's that too many other nations in your world now have that amazing destructive power. But I am also certain they would have gotten it anyway. There is no way to stop the march of science. There are only people like you: passionate, loving people who see right from wrong. Individuals who must lead your own generation toward goodness, fairness, justice and decency.

Genevieve, forgive me, if not for my actions in 1945 than for reading your diary here tonight. I read of your pain, your struggle, your victories and what now seems to be a setback. You're older than your years, but you still have the hope that only children have. It is my most sincere wish that you prevail against your cancer. I will pray for you and for your grandmother. I pray that she is well enough soon to join you in that empty bed beside you. And I pray that when that cancer is gone from your body, if a cancer is what you still view me to be, that I am the only cancer in your life ever again. All your cancers out of time. All your cancers from the past.

Humbly,

President Truman

P.S. Genevieve, when your anger subsides, please look up two men who lived in my time on earth. I think you will find what they did hopeful and in light of your current condition, fascinating. They were professors at Yale University and their names are Louis Goodman and Alfred Gilman.

OMG! Where do I start? I woke up. The room was dark. It was like maybe 4 a.m. I woke up because the room was so hot. Like what happened? Someone crank the heat before they left the room? I got up and went over to the thermostat on the wall. It looked like it was set to 74 degrees. OK, a little warm. Nothing out of the ordinary for a dopey hospital with lousy covers. But the temperature in the room said 98.6! Like body temperature? Are you kidding me? Why would anyone want the room to be body temperature?

OK Genevieve, enough with the "like" being in all your sentences. Sorry, MD, I'm a better writer than that. I'm just a little freaked out right now. And not just because the room seemed to have miraculously gone all "human body" on me. But then when I came over to pick up the nurses' buzzer and ask if someone had been in here, I saw you open to writing that wasn't mine! It wasn't my mom's either. I thought, "Well, that's rude. Whatever nurse came in here and cranked the heat must've taken the liberty of jotting notes in my diary." Then I thought, "Maybe it was my fault, though: for writing MD on the front."

So just as I started to blame myself for making the nurses think you were some medical notebook or chart or something they could write in, I read the signature! President Truman! Are you kidding me?

Nuts! This is all nuts.

Something's batty for sure around here, and I think it must be me. This is lunacy. Lunacy! Hey, that could be a little sidekick for BattyPatty. BattyPatty and her partner in crime, the ultra-crafty Luna Tick! While BattyPatty flits around tuning in on the tragic stories of the little kids who wander into my strange and amazing land of healthy kids with tiny problems, it's Luna her tick sidekick that sets about to help the kids overcome them.

Here you go little Billy. Rub my secret Luna medicine wand on that acne and your face will be beautiful and clear in time for tonight's dance!

Wait, Genevieve, focus.

Harry Truman wrote to you? Impossible. Impossible. Not

Possible. MD! Harry Truman wrote IN you? Not possible.

Look, I know you're a magic diary, but that's just a turn of a phrase. What did Mrs. Welch say? It's some trick time plays. She said there's a word for it. Temporality or something. Temporality is, as a matter of fact, an easily explained little trick the mind plays on you: making time slow down or speed up. Like when your waiting to go to the movies and time seems to drag.

But getting messages from dead presidents. That's not temporality. That's NUTS.

Nuts! I wish it wasn't so hot in here. Hey, maybe I'm dreaming. Yeah, this is just a dream. What did they put in that IV last night? Some new chemo they said. Something I've never had before. It wasn't around four years ago when I had my last medicine. That's all this is, a drug allergy. But why does the thermometer read 98.6? Oh yeah, that's part of the hallucination. I need to call the nurse.

But wait.

Before they fix me. Maybe I should just see if my **wild imagination** wrote anything any good. Ha! Yeah, I think I'll go read what Harry Truman wrote. Then I'll call the nurse.

Uh, ok, I'm back. I haven't called the nurse yet though. I know I should have her come in and flush this IV with saline, but I don't want the pages from Harry Truman to go away.

"Sure Genevieve, we can get rid of the allergic reaction but then the lovely mysterious hallucinations go away too."

I did get up and check the thermometer again and it's down to 87.2 in here. That aspect of the hallucination appears to be taking care of itself. I would make a joke about how it was "hot as hell" when President Truman was in here writing his letter. But I don't think he came from hell. At least I don't think so, anymore. I don't know what that hot temperature was all about. But I don't think it was the President's fault.

I am sorry I called you Hateful Harry, though, Mr. President. I guess I hadn't quantified the 30 thousand people dying every day. But who would? Who could? I guess if I were a better student in Mr. Murray's class, I could have just done the math. Fifty-one million people divided by the number of years and the number of days in a year. Math problems aren't like that though. Math problems are always something stupid and irrelevant. Like: Jane leaves city A at 50 miles per hour, blah blah blah.

Would kids learn better if the problems were more like real life? Of course, not like that "real life." It's too much like "real death" math problems. I mean six million Jews killed in six years! "How many does that mean died per month, little Billy?" Little Billy solves the problem and then goes to bed and cries himself to sleep. That would be awful homework. But maybe it would teach people the truth about war. And maybe people would learn to hate war. I don't know. A lot of very smart grown-ups can't figure out how to stop war. Clearly, they don't want any competition from pre-algebra class. I guess they don't want the kids in Mr. Murray's class showing them up.

Nuts.

The nurse just walked in with another bag of that chemo. She's fussing with it over by the sink. I can't let her dose me up on it if it's making me hallucinate. What if this trippy stuff just gets worse? I think I'll ask her to wake Mom up before she gives me any more of that medicine. I'll tell her it makes me itchy or something. That will stall for time until Mom gets here.

The hospital has a big couch in the family room on the eighth floor and they let my mother watch her shows out there late at night. She loves those cooking shows. She says they get her mind off things. It must work. She always falls asleep out in the family room.

Anyway, if I stall for them to go get her, Mom can decide what to tell the nurse about her daughter seeing things – and feeling things – that aren't even there. Mom will figure it out.

Or she'll flip out.

No. On second thought, I won't tell her to wake up Mom. I'll ask the nurse to come in here. And then I'll ask her to call who? I know who. Nana!

Well Nana just got off the phone with the nurse. I don't know what she said but all poop is breaking loose around here now. Did they all have to freak out so bad? I'll answer that one. No. No, they did not.

I can see giving me a new IV bag of saline, but seriously? A whole new IV? Sure, it doesn't matter to them. They aren't the ones getting stuck. What did that nurse say? They have to find out if it's the polyvinyl chloride leaching from the IV bags and other tubing used to hook me to the new medicine and not the new medicine itself.

I don't think the nurse's hypothesis makes any sense. I told her so too. She was telling this junk to mom when I interrupted and said, "I've gotten IVs as long as I can remember, and it never happened before. Why now?" At first, she looked at me like I was crazy, and I can tell she was just going to dismiss me. And mom just looked terrified. But that's when Nana came in.

I guess I don't have to tell you, MD. I've never been so happy to see anyone IN MY LIFE. Nana said, "Sounds like a good question, Genevieve." And then she asked the nurse the same question herself.

Nothing worse than an old lady in a wheelchair pushing herself into a conversation. I smiled at her and hollered, "Nana, you're in a wheelchair?"

Nana just smiled back and said, "My left side was still a smidge weak. But my sass is as strong as ever." Then she winked at me.

Man, I love that wink. Nana's just fine.

Anyway, the nurse then explained to Nana that they've found that this polyvinyl chloride junk can accumulate. So far, they've only found it to be a problem in tiny babies. But compromised immune systems are what they are, and they wanted to make sure. I guess that's why they had me pee in a cup again too. To see if the junk was being filtered by my kidneys. I almost asked if they were sure the cups weren't made of that polyvinyl stuff. But before I could, they handed me a paper cup.

Everyone, and I mean everyone, in the room was sweating

too. Although it felt much better than when I first woke up. I think someone turned the air conditioning on to cool it off.

After they were all done getting their tests done and rewiring my fluid delivery system, Nana asked everyone to leave us alone. She even kicked Mom out. Oh, she was nice about it. She rubbed Mom's hand, and whispered, "Rachel, go home. You look like you haven't slept in a week. Let me take a shift here with my favorite granddaughter and you get some rest. I'll call you if they come back with any answers."

I told Mom I was worried about her too. And besides, if she went home, she could bring me back a mocha milkshake from the Dairy Dream near our house. Finally, she agreed. Once she had something she could do for someone else, she was on her way.

When the room was quiet, Nana turned and said, "Now let me see this magic diary of yours."

I still don't know what she told the nurse about my hallucinations, but she definitely left out the part about the diary and the dead president.

I handed you over and Nana – just like an old eighth floor pro – gently slid her right hand under my IV hand. (I had to beg them not to put the new IV into my writing hand. I blamed it on homework. But it was all about you!) And with you in her lap, Nana began to read. I told her she only needed to read the end. But she said she wanted to read from the beginning. I was a little nervous about her reading all the things I had written about her, and Mom, and Dad. But after a while the room got quiet and I drifted off to sleep.

When I woke up Nana was sitting there staring at you on the tray table. I told her, "Hi." And she responded, "Genevieve, I don't know what the doctors will decide about the medicine or the vinyl stuff in the IV bags. And I don't care. I think Harry Truman wrote to you and I think you should do what he told you to do. When you get the rest of your homework done, I want you to look up those scientists from Yale and see why they are so important."

I don't think Nana bought the notion of a dead President Truman writing to me. I think she saw this as a great diversion from all the other things a relapsed cancer kid has to worry about. But one thing was for sure. The words were still there. Nana had read them. She knew about the guys from Yale and that part, at least, wasn't a hallucination.

I smiled at her. She winked at me. And then Mom walked in with two giant milkshakes!

After dinner I finished my homework. Nana asked Mom if we could use her iPad. Of course, Mom said, "Yes." And then she scurried off to the family room to watch three or four chefs trying to outdo each other while making something disgusting with squid or cow tongue, or both. Gag!

When the coast was clear, Nana and I looked up Drs. Louis S. Goodman and Alfred Gilman. Turned out there was more than one famous Dr. Gilman. Alfred had a son who won a Nobel prize for something or other in biology. Nana said he had good genes. I'm sure you won't be surprised to learn Nana always says I have good genes too, on account of her and Mom. I always smile when she says that. But I think I'd smile a little more if I didn't get cancer. Some of that is genetic too.

I suppose she could say the bad cells come from my dad's side. And they **probably do**. With all her high blood pressure and other stuff, at least Nana's never had cancer. Good genes from Mom. Bad cells from Dad.

Anyway, these two guys Goodman and Gilman were pharmacologists at Yale University. Way back in the early 1940's they worked on finding chemicals to fix people when they got sick. So, yeah, President Truman was right. They were around when he was around. He had to be president to know about them, because all their work was top secret on account of the war.

From what Nana and I read, doctors – back in those days – weren't really expected to do very much with medicines. Most of the major health benefits – back then – were from surgery or radiation. The x-ray machine wasn't even 50 years old in 1942 but they were already using radiation to fight cancer. Another good thing about an x-ray was that it could tell the surgeon where a tumor was, so he could cut it out.

I've never had surgery or radiation for my cancer. It's weird to think my medicines are so new. I find it remarkable my cancer treatments aren't even as old as my Nana. But I think that's why President Truman wanted me to learn about these guys.

I know. It wasn't Truman. A dead president couldn't tell me to look up Goodman and Gilman: or tell me to look up **any**thing for that matter.

I don't care.

Nana says just to say President Truman wrote a letter and leave it alone. It's easier than saying my hallucination wanted me to look up two scientists. Anyway, Nana thinks maybe I wrote it to myself and can't remember doing it. I don't know. Seems like my hand would be tired.

But again, it doesn't matter. It wasn't just that my medicine has been around for less than 80 years that amazed me. It was that my medicine hasn't always been medicine. Before Goodman and Gilman got their hands on it, it had a different purpose. IT WAS A WEAPON!

No kidding. Long before the chemicals in chemotherapy saved people's lives, governments sprayed those same chemicals on battlefields to kill each other's soldiers.

And all that killing was the real reason for the research. Scientists do a lot of research. And these two guys had been reading the autopsies of men in World War I who **died** because a chemical got sprayed on them. The chemical was called mustard gas. If a guy wasn't wearing a gas mask when he got exposed to mustard gas, then he died pretty fast. But this poison could seep through someone's skin too. And if a guy was wearing a mask but got it on his skin, he'd still die, but it would take weeks.

So back in 1942, Goodman and Gilman worked for the War Department trying to find an antidote to mustard gas in case anyone tried using it on people in World War II. Their work was top secret.

Goodman and Gilman (GG from now on) figured out that the guys who took a while dying had like no white blood cells left. Well, a few. But not enough to keep them alive anymore.

Anyway, the chemical agent in the mustard gas that killed the white blood cells (I looked it up again, they're called lymphocytes and leukocytes) is nitrogen mustard. Anyway, these two smart guys knew that lots of cancer patients who have blood cancer died because their blood supply was filling up with mutated cells.

Mutated cells are cells that don't work the way they should. Or they reproduce over and over again. Nobody can shut them off. But even if they could, nobody knew how get rid of all the mutated blood cells that accumulated in someone's body.

Think about it, MD, no surgeon could cut out the bad blood cells one at a time. And even though radiation could mess with some of the bad cells, it didn't work on these blood cancers for very long. More importantly, radiation didn't work at all on some of the cancers. GG wondered if this nitrogen mustard could work on – wait for it magic diary – lymphoma and leukemia!

Now you know why President Truman wanted me to know all this. Because leukemia, what I have, was first treated with a weapon that had killed thousands of people in a war.

I flipped! I kept repeating, "Holy Crud" and "Awe Nuts" to Nana and she told me to stop looking this stuff up. But I didn't want to stop. I couldn't stop. I wasn't angry. I was, like, WOW! People died and because of their deaths and because GG studied them: their deaths saved lives!

But Nana got worried about me reading about all these people dying from cancer. She wanted me to stop. It is scary to think about all the tragedy in the world. And senseless cruelty like the two world wars. But it's fascinating to learn how people change because of all these terrible circumstances.

So, I reminded Nana of what I had already written in this here diary. I reminded her of what she had already read.

MD, just 'cause we don't talk about me dying of leukemia, doesn't mean I don't think about it. And besides this information blew my mind and I understood why President Truman wanted me to understand that not everything was all good and not everything was all bad. He wanted me to understand HIM a little bit better.

So anyway, these smart scientists tried the mustard nitrogen on sick mice and the mice got better. Their work was still top secret and they still hadn't found an antidote to the mustard gas, but they were getting closer to finding the first chemical cure for cancer. So secretly GG looked for a cancerous human to test mustard nitrogen on, someone who could be trusted.

Oh, the story was wonderful. They found this man who was so sick with blood cancer he couldn't lay down, swallow or sleep. He couldn't put his arms all the way down because his back and front were full of tumors and swollen cancerous lymph nodes. They gave the guy – they called him JD – a dose of the nitrogen mustard and he got better. They gave him another dose and he got better again! After a while he was eating and sleeping and moving around with more comfort.

Sadly, mustard nitrogen was new and so experimental that they couldn't control the side effects or know how much to give him. The procedures caused new problems. The more medicine JD got, the more damage it did to healthier parts of his body. GG tried to give him blood transfusions. My doctors have given me those before, when there's so much chemotherapy in me that it's killing me and not the cancer. Transfusions have worked for me, but they didn't work for JD. And after a while, 96 days after it all started, JD lost his battle with cancer.

JD died in December of 1942. He was a Polish immigrant. And the whole thing is even more prophetic now because I know Harry S Truman better. It's amazing that cancer killed JD in America while Hitler was brutally killing his Polish countrymen back in Poland.

Hitler was the cancer, not Truman. I don't hate Truman anymore. Not one bit.

I told Nana about that. She told me that President Truman lived in a very complicated time. "And, speaking of time," she said, "Time for bed."

Nana wants to trade me Kazzu for you, MD. She wants me to go to sleep and I told her I was putting you under my pillow, so nobody messed with you again. She doesn't want me to sleep with you under my pillow. I held my ground. She didn't look happy, but I wore her down.

Nana told me, "Fine." There she sat, one hand on her hip, wagging the index finger of her other hand at me and ranting, "But tomorrow I'm going to teach your teacher a thing or two about giving a little sick kid such depressing reading assignments."

I told her, "Not so fast, Nana, I'm not a little kid anymore. And that last reading assignment wasn't even from my teachers. So yeah, good luck with that."

Nana looked shocked, and then she winked at me. Good night Nana. Good night MD.

Well, I woke up this morning and the thermometer in the room read 73.8 degrees. I don't know what I thought. I guess I even hoped that it would be hot in here again and I'd open you up and find a note from JD or something. I guess I kind of hoped he'd tell me his cancer story. Oh well. All a dream.

Maybe I'm just lonely.

Nana went off to the school to meet with Mr. Dunsten and Mrs. Welch and anyone else who would talk to her about making homework a little less depressing. One thing is for sure, that stroke isn't slowing her down anymore. She hired a nice lady named Alma who comes and helps her get dressed and drives her places now.

Anyway, Nana's gone with Alma and Mom's at work. My mom teaches accounting at a small women's college. I know, right! Who would have thought my worried-all-the-time mom would have a cool head for numbers? She used to work for the state as an auditor. But when I got sick – half my lifetime ago – she decided she needed something that wasn't so 9 to 5. Mom says she "can grade papers in my hospital room," but, "can't sit at a desk in the capitol and keep an eye on me."

Today, she's got student office hours and teaches two 90-minute classes, so she'll be gone awhile.

I know one thing, MD! I'm not going anywhere!

Dr. Borlasa came in early this morning before mom and Nana even left. She said they decided to put me back on that new medicine. Dr. Borlasa explained, "I'm fairly certain the feeling hot and seeing flying bats with earrings has nothing to do with the chemicals that make up your IV tubes and bags." And if it was the new medicine? "Well," she said, "Even if it caused irregularities, every drug has side effects. I think we can handle a few imaginary friends for a while if it means we get rid of the new cancer."

When Dr. Borlasa said, "Imaginary friends," you know that Nana winked at me! Sometimes she makes it hard to keep a straight face.

One thing's for sure. Nana toned the story down. She told them I was seeing things but stuck to the imaginary stuff I'd already talked about for years like BattyPatty and Luna the tick sidekick. Stuff I've created to think about every time I get scared. Good old Nana left out the dead president crossing over to argue his war criminal defense in the court of Genevieve.

"Your honor, the defense would like to call its first witness in Genevieve's *mentalcourt.*" BattyPatty can be the judge and Luna can be the defense attorney. The jury will be made of 12 tattered giraffes: Kazzu and all her friends. "The defense would like to point out, your honor, a jury of tattered giraffes is highly irregular." Then BattyPatty will gavel Luna down and reply, "Well the court would like to point out that testimony from a dead president is highly irregular as well. You may proceed."

Anyway, this morning I got all hooked up again. So here I'll stay, waiting for my hair to fall out – again. I guess I could do more homework. I have a whole bunch of math problems I haven't even touched. Mom left her iPad again, so I can listen to music while I cypher. (That's what Nana calls it. Cyphering. I don't know why: to be silly I think). Anyway, music doesn't interfere with me concentrating on math.

As Pythagoras once said, "There is geometry in the humming of the strings, there is music in the spacing of the spheres." The way Mr. Murray tells it, Pythagoras understood the relationship between music and math. Mr. Murray told us Pythagoras – the Greek mathematician every kid hates for explaining how to figure the length of missing sides on right triangles – also explained harmony. After walking by a metal smith clanging on an anvil, Pythagoras used mathematics to create something called the diatonic scale. He hung spheres from cords. And voila! Chords!

Mr. Murray thought we'd like him better if we knew he did something cool. Mom used to tell me I couldn't listen to music and do homework. Then I hit her with Mr. Murray's Pythagorean harmony theory, and she relented.

So yeah, music and math. Listening can be tough when I'm reading. Hearing song lyrics jumbles my words. The words in my ears mix up inside my head with the words from my eyes.

What, you ask, am I listening too?

Ever since I was a little kid, I loved Nat King Cole. I know, right? What's a gal like me doing with a musical fascination from the Jazz Era? I mean, he'd be a hundred years old or something by now. As usual, you can just blame Nana.

When I was first diagnosed, Nana would bring her VCR into the hospital and play his videos for me. One day I woke up singing a bunch of his lyrics. Mom said I fell in love with Nat King Cole's music somewhere in my dreams.

Back in the day – my first hospital days – Nana assured me Nat King Cole's smooth voice lulled her to sleep for decades and he'd lull me to sleep too. Don't get me wrong, plenty of nights ended with me hearing his soft smooth melodies or old jazz recordings. But he sang peppy songs too. Songs like "Straighten Up and Fly Right." Nana fancied herself a good dancer and when that song came on, she'd start dancing around the hospital room (if I was sick) or our kitchen back home (when I got better) and make me giggle for a solid three and a half minutes.

One time, in the throes of a faux tap dance routine, Nana threatened, "Someday I'm going to sing this song to your Dad, Genevieve. Think he'll get the hint?" Mom stormed out of the room. Nana never mentioned that particular idea again.

Speaking of lousy ideas, here comes the phlebotomist. Argh! A yick and a stick.

D ear Genevieve,

I saw you here sleeping with your headphones. I can hear you listening to Nat King Cole singing one of his favorite songs. I wrote that song. It's called, "Smile." I composed the music for my motion picture, Modern Times, in 1936. Eighteen years later two lyricists, John Turner and Geoffrey Parsons set words to the tune and Nat King Cole, a thirty-five-year-old jazz phenomenon, released the first recording of the song the same year.

Since then some of the brightest stars in the music industry sang "Smile" for their adoring fans. Perhaps you've heard Barbra Streisand's version or the one sung by the legendary Tony Bennett. If you have not, ask your Nana, she'll know how to find them.

I wonder if any of these immortal music icons would have crooned my tune if not for Nat King Cole – the black man born in the segregated south – singing it first. Nat made "Smile" a smash hit!

I was one month shy of my twentieth birthday when Nathaniel Adams Cole was born in Birmingham, Alabama on St. Patrick's Day 1919.

I covered a lot of ground in those twenty years before Nat's arrival on the scene. I worked very hard. Born in London, my dad ran off when I was little. I know you know how that feels.

Although she suffered from poor health, my mom toiled long hours to provide for us. Hard as she tried, my mom couldn't make enough to pay our bills, I went off to a work house when I was nine-years-old.

When I turned 14, they locked my mother away in a hospital for the insane – a prison for the mentally ill. Regardless of what you call it, it was society's segregation of people it couldn't help or didn't understand. A place for... what do you call them? Batty people. Science didn't have much to offer the batty in those days. I'm not surprised they couldn't cure her back then and I doubt caging her improved her condition.

In my teen years, I sang and performed. I wanted a better

life. I believed in myself. I wanted a life without misery, and I wanted to make other people, well, like my song says: I wanted them to smile. I performed on stage after stage. My years of hard work paid off. I got a contract singing and acting with a company that brought me to the United States. My unique brand of humor captivated audiences. Not afraid to test limits, I dressed up in costumes and used pantomime to tell stories. Motion Pictures – a new invention in my day – captured the fascination and imagination of ordinary people. When I changed my garb, I communicated to millions in these captive audiences through the characters I invented. The most popular of these was a hobo. I called him, "The Little Tramp."

By the time I turned 29, I was one of the best-known performers in the world. This too is true of Nat. He and his King Cole Trio dazzled the music scene. My fame grew because of how I looked, Nat's celebrity grew in spite of his appearance. Racism in 1940's America stunted the careers of black men in the music business. But the music business had not met many men – regardless of color – like Nat King Cole.

Nat began his career performing jazz with other musicians. But his voice – his perfect pitch and smooth delivery – made him a household name. Sometimes, fame grips a man and throws him in front of the world: in front of an imperfect world. A black man with talent, poise and dignity threatens an imperfect world by flaunting his gifts to the weaker around him.

I must tell you dear Genevieve, it's unmanageable to have it all, to become a successful legend in your own lifetime. Because even as millions adore you, it's impossible to keep others from hating you. Once someone hates you, he or she can't forget you. Many seek to destroy what they hate. Many try to obliterate what they can't get out of their heads. Before long, they act on their desire to eliminate you and they plot your demise.

Genevieve, I know that you have studied World War II in school this year.

While I climbed to the top of my fame and popularity, Adolf Hitler grew powerful in Europe. He became the leader of one of Europe's largest countries. Hitler elevated some by destroying others. Many people looked the other way. So many people did, in fact, that Hitler and his maniacs reigned terror and misery on hundreds of millions of people before the combined forces across six continents could stop him.

People in the United States heard how Hitler stampeded across Europe. They read that he oppressed the Jews and forced them to live in Ghettos. But oppression and segregation flourished in the U.S. as well. When Nat was born, his parents lived in the segregated south. Colored people couldn't sit on a train with a white person or drink from the same water fountain. Lynchings were commonplace. Many in the U.S. embraced eugenics. They believed in the phony bologna science that claimed some people were – by virtue of their physical characteristics – better than others. Eugenicists labeled certain populations inferior and demanded their numbers be controlled, much the way sterilization and extermination are the answer to perceived infestations of other kinds.

At five years of age, Nat's parents, wanting a better life for their son, moved him from the segregated south to Chicago, Illinois. They tried to distance him from the racism and bigotry they'd encountered all their lives. Early twentieth century America didn't have regional racism. American had racism by degree. It existed all across the nation – as the Nat would learn as he grew.

Eleven years after Hitler's racist extermination campaign ended, On the 10th of April 1956, a group of white supremacists stormed the stage during one of Nat's performances in Birmingham, Alabama and attempted to kidnap him. They beat him brutally. According to eyewitnesses, plain clothed policemen tried to help Nat, but they were repelled by the uniformed officers who were on duty at the time. Nat survived the attack with pain from his injuries that would last the rest of his life.

Later that year, Nat King Cole became the first African American to have a nationwide television program. Not one single company would sponsor the show's cross-country broadcast. No one wanted to insult the white racists by putting a black man into their living rooms.

It's almost unthinkable that this could have happened AF-TER Adolf Hitler. Humanity still has much to learn from our failings. Even today, Genevieve, your 21st century news headlines are filled with hatred and murder based on color, religion, race.

Hitler's tactics worked in our day as they work in yours, Genevieve. In the 1930s the U.S. had become isolationist. American bankers had loaned immense fortunes to Great Britain and France so they could fight the First World War and by the time Hitler went goose-stepping across Europe, those banks still held vast European debt. Behind the scenes wealthy lenders wanted the U.S. to mind its own business and leave this war in Europe to the Europeans – at least until those nations paid their bills.

Hitler used propaganda to control people. We saw it. People in my industry saw it. We knew the power of our films. We knew we had the ability to whip up human sentiment against Hitler. Somehow, despite all that knowledge, even after Hitler invaded Poland and annexed Austria, the U.S. film industry remained neutral. My industry cowed as Nat's NBC studio cowed when confronted by the bullies in America.

The film industry, **my colleagues**, stayed silent. Even though many of my showbiz peers were Jews they didn't mention German atrocities in their pictures.

When the United States government limited the number of Jewish people who could emigrate to safety, the Warner Brothers and many others purchased visas for displaced Jews and sponsored their passage to freedom. But the tariffs to the U.S. government were high and in the long run they helped only a few. These film makers with the power to speak to millions worked in silence and on a miniscule scale.

I knew we had to do more. I knew we had to use our movies, or public relations power, to do something. Maybe it wouldn't work. Still, we had to try.

Nations across the globe struggled to recover from the Great Depression of 1929. Hitler's German economy surged forward. In the United States, before the second world war began, Hitler was praised for rebuilding Germany. Popular magazines across the free world put his face on the cover. U.S. heroes (like the famous pilot pioneer, Charles Lindbergh) praised him.

It seemed the American people were befuddled and didn't know what to believe when Great Britain and France declared war on Germany. Vast numbers of U.S. immigrants had come from Germany and their ally, Italy. These people didn't want the U.S. to go to war and drop bombs on their cousins, parents, and friends back home.

Oh Genevieve, alliances, family ties, and fear confused people.

I knew the film makers had to take the lead. I knew we had to use our film industry to push back against this false prophet. We had to quell the fear. I grew up Episcopalian, but Hitler called me a pseudo-Jew. He used the name to insult me and to discredit my work. I felt like I had a badge of honor. In some sick and twisted way, Hitler had recognized me as an ally to his prey. I became a target of his and anyone who didn't want me ruffling the feathers of American isolationism.

Back in 1939 and 1940, dear Genevieve, I felt more alone than I can describe. But I knew I was right. So, I made a film, *The Great Dictator*. I dressed up as Hitler. I made fun of him and his "land of the double cross." I made fun of his desire to rule the world. Unlike Hitler, the absurd human spectacle exposed in my movie turned around and my "Great Dictator" renounced despotism. Here is what he said:

"I'm sorry, but I don't want to be an emperor. That's not my business. I don't want to rule or conquer anyone. I should like to help everyone - if possible - Jew, Gentile - black man - white. We all want to help one another. Human beings are like that. We want to live by each other's happiness - not by each other's misery. We don't want to hate and despise one another. In this world there is room for everyone. And the good earth is rich and can provide for everyone. The way of life can be free and beautiful, but we have lost the way.

"Greed has poisoned men's souls, has barricaded the world

with hate, has goose-stepped us into misery and bloodshed. We have developed speed, but we have shut ourselves in. Machinery that gives abundance has left us in want. Our knowledge has made us cynical. Our cleverness, hard and unkind. We think too much and feel too little. More than machinery we need humanity. More than cleverness we need kindness and gentleness. Without these qualities, life will be violent, and all will be lost....

"The aeroplane and the radio have brought us closer together. The very nature of these inventions cries out for the goodness in men - cries out for universal brotherhood - for the unity of us all. Even now my voice is reaching millions throughout the world - millions of despairing men, women, and little children - victims of a system that makes men torture and imprison innocent people."

Genevieve, great performers should never become great informers unless they want their careers, or their reputations destroyed. In the 1950's there was a great American inquisition.

You know what I mean by an inquisition, don't you, Genevieve? When people act out of fear and hunt for a boogie man, a scapegoat, someone to pin their darkest fears on and then to destroy. Somehow, they believed that by crushing greatness in others, they could vindicate themselves in front of all their imaginary demons. Hitler and his inquisitors hunted Jews and Gypsies, Jehovah's Witnesses and conscientious objectors, the innocent and their children. After great loss of life and treasure, a horrified world stopped that madness. Bullies across the globe learned from Hitler's miscalculations. The next grand inquisitors learned that they had to be more subjective, less obvious.

In the 1950's the inquisition hunted Communists. When they couldn't find them, they invented them. Then they set out to destroy them. The U.S. Federal Bureau of Investigation under the leadership of the fanatic, J. Edgar Hoover, attacked me and others like me. They targeted great people (Helen Keller to name one!) whose only crime was speaking out in defense of the poor.

(Genevieve, I only hope that Helen Keller takes time to tell you her story).

Unlike Miss. Keller, I was not an American citizen. And though Hoover tried to expel me from the United States, he never could. Instead, he conspired with the immigration officials of the time and denied me re-entry when I left to work in Europe.

Genevieve, here is part of the statement I made to the press:

"Since the end of the last world war, I have been the object of lies and propaganda by powerful reactionary groups who, by their influence and by the aid of America's yellow press, have created an unhealthy atmosphere in which liberal-minded individuals can be singled out and persecuted. Under these conditions I find it virtually impossible to continue my motion-picture work, and I have therefore given up my residence in the United States."

Move from my dogged resistance to Nat King Cole's courage in those same years. He saw crosses burned on his lawn. He sang in segregated music halls and faced persecution for the color of his skin.

Try as we did, in the end, the bad guys won. Hoover banished me from the U.S. and Nat gave in to public pressure.

On Christmas day in 1964 Nat's eldest daughter, Carole, gave birth to a baby girl. Carole – Cookie as her parents called her – was not married. Her white boyfriend, the father of the baby, did not interfere when Cookie's parents demanded she give the baby to an adoption agency.

One of the wealthiest black members of the music industry, Nat and his family lived in a 20-room house, but they didn't have room for a baby.

Success is part of life. Failure is part of life. For a life well lived, giving up is not an option. Trite as it sounds, we did the best we could.

Genevieve, I hope you and I become better acquainted as you move forward in your journey. Perhaps your Nana would download some of my movies onto your mom's iPad. You can watch them the same way you listened as Nat King Cole sang you to sleep.

Until then, have many more "sweet dreams," Genevieve. Like the ones your mom talked about. The ones that allowed you to fall in love with the talent and the message of one decent, honorable jazz singer.

I know you have challenges ahead. You've faced so many already. But as you've already found "Life is still worthwhile, if you just... Smile,"

Charlie Chaplin

Hey Charlie,

Thanks for the kind words. One thing I'd like to add about me and my family: I shudder to think of my granddaughter going through challenges like yours, Genevieve. I didn't do any thing to keep an eye on her after we gave her away. But then, of course, I died of lung cancer two months after the adoption. My wife though, she always worried that we had abandoned her to an unsafe fate. When the little girl was 12, my Maria hosted a sleep over at her apartment in New York City. The event seemed random, but our granddaughter was among the invited guests. Maria confirmed our hopes that our granddaughter had a good family and a happy childhood. Good things for a grandmother to know. They never saw each other again.

Best of luck Genevieve,
Nat

I woke up so thirsty. At first, I thought, "this chemo is dehydrating me more than last time." Then I thought, "Either it's the chemo or how stinking hot it is in here."

My eyes flew open! Hot? I jumped out of bed and ran to the wall thermostat.

I couldn't make it all the way over to the wall mount because I forgot to bring the IV pole along. But I got close enough to read the lighted display on the electronic register. Sure enough: 95 degrees! Not as hot as last time, but still **doggone hot**. And nowhere near normal temperature for a hospital room with climate control.

I rushed back to the bed. I pulled my pillow off and there underneath it – just where I left you – you sat. One little magic diary looking intact. At least I thought you looked unmolested until I looked where I left off. But the writing didn't end where I left off. No, Charlie Chaplin – **of course! Who else?** MD, silent movie stars are at the top of everyone's hit parade to come back from the dead and talk to teenagers! Charlie Chaplin had been beckoned to comment by my listening to Nat King Cole music! Thanks Nana!

"Your honor, the defense would like to call Charlie Chaplin." BattyPatty responds, "There is no one here by that name."

"Well, your honor," responds Luna, "We'll need **an** ethereal auditory subpoena please." BattyPatty gavels the room to attention, "We will stand adjourned until Charlie Chaplin appears."

What a nice touch to have Nat King Cole tag along to thank him for his testimony. Must be all the time those two guys spent sticking up for justice over the years.

OK, OK, I'm making jokes. But **seriously**. I'm **starting to think** there's something **super** strange going on here. I'm thinking I might be even a little bit angry about all these posts in MY diary. It's not nice to mess with the head of a kid with cancer.

I called the nurse, I asked her for my mom and my

grandmother. Had they come back? She said, "No, it's only 2:25 p.m. You fell asleep about noon. I closed the blinds in your room, and it's been quiet since."

This is messed up. I fell asleep in the middle of the day and this happened again. Last time it was at night. Still taking the medicine though. Except Nana could read what President Truman wrote last time. So, it's not pure hallucination. Argh.

The nurse spoke again, "Joe the physical therapist is here to take you down to work on the medicine ball."

Well, that's a weird name - if ever I heard one - for exercise equipment. What do I do with you, MD? Take you with me?

It was almost like Joe read my mind. "Hey," he says, "I see you're writing like crazy in that book. Just bring it with. That way you can use it if we have to wait for the equipment."

Yeah, it's not like a freaking-out teen can skip her physical therapy. Joe the mind reader strikes again, "You don't want lymphedema or some other annoying physical complication to get the better of you, do you?"

You mean like poor JD from 1942? I thought about asking Joe if he ever heard of the first chemo patient and his gigantic lymph nodes. Then I thought the better of it. I'd just go along with Joe and bring MD along for safe keeping.

"Good idea. Thanks Joe." I managed to sound normal and not overwrought. (How old is Joe? Like 24? Sometimes I wonder if these guys who aren't much older than me pity me. It doesn't matter, I guess. He's nice to my face).

"Besides," he said, "I gotta get you out of here. It's like a sauna in here."

I'm back and so is my grandmother. Nana got back here with a milkshake and one of Charlie Chaplin's smiles on her face.

I guess Mrs. Welch and Mr. Dunsten learned a thing or two. At least Nana felt like she made some ground. But after I read Mrs. Welch's letter, I got the idea that they pretty much all felt the same way from the minute they found out about my reaction to the nuclear bombing of Japan. Making a scared little kid scareder (Yeah, I know it's not a word) – anyway – scaring a scared kid doesn't seem very nice.

The milkshake was yummy. Joe had just brought me back to the room when Nana rolled back in too. Alma pushed the wheelchair and Nana held the milkshakes for the three of us in a cup holder on her lap. "Oh Joe! Good to see you," she beamed. I knew at once from that excited tone, Nana had been triumphant at school. "If I'd known you were going to be here, I'd have brought you your favorite strawberry milkshake!" Joe seemed flattered that she remembered his favorite flavor but said, "No worries, Nana." Yeah, Nana allowed him to call her that. I even think she liked it. Then Joe patted his flat tummy and said, "I'm watching my waistline since I turned 30."

"Bah," Nana replied. "30 ain't nothing. You can still drink all the dairy delights you want." And then she tossed him a victory wink.

Nana asked me how physical therapy went. I told her Joe gave me a good work out. It's not about the lymphedema or anything else medical at this point. It's just that 14-year-old girls – or anybody for that matter – shouldn't lay around all day. So, the exercise felt good but tiring.

She handed me the letter from Mrs. Welch. I'll tape it here:

H ello Genevieve,

I hope this note finds you feeling better. We miss you here and the whole school is anxious for your return.

Mr. Dunsten and I had a nice long talk with your grandma. She's quite concerned about the toll your U.S. History unit is taking on your peace of mind. She said learning about how the War in the Pacific ended had upset you. I've got to tell you that being troubled by World War II, any part of it, is a sign of good mental health. The useless suffering and almost limitless tragedy of that war is overwhelming. It had a troubling effect on many of the kids in class. Truth be told, I worry about the kids that don't get bothered by all that violence and cruelty. Either they didn't do the homework, or they lack the empathy needed to mature into happy healthy adults.

That said, we agree with your grandma. The fact that you have so many extra challenges just now must be figured into the assignments you do for the next month or so. How do you feel about doing a little Art History? Or some history of scientific discovery? I'm sending a few books along with your grandma to the hospital. Take a look and we can discuss them when I see you on Friday.

Your grandma says you love your journal. I'm glad to hear that. Perhaps you'll let me look at some of your writing when I see you?

Happy Wednesday!

Mrs. Welch

Oh great. She wants to see you. Good work Nana. Maybe I can get Nana to go buy one that looks like you before Mrs. Welch gets here and I can write some junk in it. Pull the old "switcheroo."

New assignment, huh? Scientific discovery, aye? You mean like the invention of chemotherapy? I did enjoy learning about that. I'll have to check out the books she sent after dinner. For now, Joe told me he's got a half hour break and they have a new gaming console in the family room. I think I'll go see if I can kick his butt at *War Craft!*

Nana scared the living daylights out of me last night. She said Mom wanted to read "Genevieve's new preoccupation," and so Nana decided she had to hide it. I had gone down to play *War Craft* with Joe. When I came back from the family room, Nana was gone and you were gone with her, MD.

I got panicky and then I started crying. I don't know why I cried but that was all it took and in seconds Mom was crying too. Those heartbroken eyes of hers just cracked wide open and: whoosh. We hugged each other a long time. It didn't make me less worried about losing what now seems to be a truly MAGIC DIARY, but it sure made me feel better to be that close to Mom. Let's face it, all this relapse information is bad news. And while I've been pre-occupied with world leaders and historic events, poor Mom sits immersed in my illness and without anything to distract her from her fears. Fears she experiences in real time, today.

Today.

Today. Well, yeah here's what it's like today. It's not just about medicine, procedures, or cures. No, you need to sit down with the hospital social worker and figure out how you'll pay for all of this.

"If your kid's bad news doesn't get you down Mrs. Flynn, then we've got a mountain of insurance paperwork to crush your mortal soul."

After Mom dried her eyes and then held her breath six or seven times trying to get rid of the hiccups that invariably accompany her crying jags (that's what Dad used to call them, crying jags) she explained she didn't mind filling out forms. She said all the new medical paperwork was a good thing. She said over the last few years the insurance laws had changed and **HealthyNow** couldn't deny my claims anymore. And – just as important – they couldn't max out my benefits. Mom said if I had to get sick, I picked the right time. She said since the new president took over, the U.S. Congress could be changing those laws back again. And then relapsed cancer kids like me won't be able to get treatment anymore: "Unless they're Rich!"

So yeah, panic subsided after our talk. And anyway, I knew Nana had you. And so, I trusted Nana to safeguard you, MD. Even if I was still a little petrified.

Even though, I do realize it's not possible to be "a little" petrified.

Anyway, I took a few deep breaths. I calmed myself down. I enjoyed my time alone with mom. You know, Mom seems a little different this time. Maybe it's because I'm older and I have lots of things to do. With me preoccupied by homework and dead presidents, there's less burden on her to act happy all the time. She doesn't need to keep me busy or calm. Althhough I think even as a little kid, I was more calm then she's ever been.

Still Nana says, "back in the day" my mom took a lot more stuff "in stride."

Maybe Mom's doing better this time because she's not trying to save her marriage while she's trying to save her kid. I don't know what it is. I worry about her. But, even though I still tiptoe around the cancer issues, I feel less uncertainty about her. She seems breakable still, but not as broken.

Or maybe it's me. Maybe I'm old enough to "get it." I understand that she's got to face all this grim news about her daughter. I'm not a clueless little kid anymore. I can't ignore that she's facing the toughest thing a mom can face, and I can't pretend she's not frightened. I, better than anyone, know she's frightened. She knows I could die, and I know she needs time to process that.

Nuts. I'm back. I stopped writing for about twenty minutes. I saw what I wrote and then I couldn't write any more for a little bit. Because... I don't think I've ever had this candid a conversation with myself about this DAMNED CANCER. It's what it is, MD. It's a damned disease that kills people, and I can't think about it without cussing at it. Damn damn damn.

I could die. I could die! Cease to exist. Croak. Perish. Expire. Game over. And then what? Rot? Oh no. I hope my mom never thinks about that. I hope she never lets her mind wander that far. Never ever.

No wonder she's such a mess about everything. That's a disgusting thing to think about anyone. Especially someone you love. Especially your little girl.

I don't want to die. I don't want to rot. I don't want to decompose.

There it's out in the open. It's gross. And the only good thing about it is that I won't be able to feel it. Not like now.

Now: When my blood gets thick with poison and I'm low on the good stuff.

Now: When my platelets and red blood cells vanish.

Now: When my skin peels.

Now: When my fingernails change color.

Now: When my hair falls out.

No, when I decompose in the ground, at least I'll be dead.

But, with luck, not soon. Not soon for my sake and not soon for my mom's sake.

There, now that this is off my chest, I should be able to think about other things. 'Cause it's time to get back to writing about my day! No more composing about decomposing! Ha Ha. Bet you didn't think I could joke about dying. Fooled you! You spend a little more time on the eighth floor, MD, and you'll hear lots of jokes about things that nobody else thinks are funny.

It's how we Americans cope.

I saw that on some talk show with Nana one time. Other cultures wail and cry and beat their chests. Americans use sick humor. The news story showed pictures of people in other countries laying on the coffin of their loved ones – inside a grave! I don't want any of that when I die. Just a few jokes please.

Nana told me that when her Uncle John died, they gathered in the funeral home and stayed late. She said the funeral director walked in a "few sheets to the wind" and told everyone, that if they weren't lying down, they'd have to leave! Well, of course, only Uncle John could stay. She said everyone laughed and got their coats.

Imagine, making someone laugh at a funeral parlor.

Enough of that. Now that we're smiling again, on with the next story. Positive thoughts, MD. That will help and I got a doozie of a story to tell you.

Here goes.

Once upon a time: Nana came back after dinner with a "friend" Mrs. Mattingly. I could tell as soon as they walked in the room that Mom had never met her. Mom gets kind of stiff and awkward when someone new comes into her sick kid's hospital room.

Nana told mom she'd met Mrs. Mattingly in the rehab hospital that Nana went to after her stroke. She told mom, "Mrs. Mattingly loves to play cards. I invited her to come play here, with me, while I sit with Genevieve and you go watch your chefs wrestle with some filo dough."

Mom smiled and said hello to the lady. She had that "if you say so" look on her face.

Mom hugged me and held on for a good long while. She told me she loved me, and you know I told her the same. It had been a good cry, a productive cry. One we both needed. Her weeping was mixed full of "don't you dare take my baby away from me" waterworks and my cry left "those poor children from Hiroshima" and "holy Hannah, I'm hallucinating" tears all over the back of her shirt.

Mom shook hands with the lady and walked out of the room. Mom mouthed, "I love you," again at me from the doorway. My sweet mom looked reluctant to go, but she knew we were both a lot better off after that little time alone with each other.

Nana may be the one teaching a-thing-or-two to everyone, but mom is the one rooted in reality so deep, she pulls pain up from the earth's core and it makes her trunk as strong as the sequoia in my environmental sciences book.

We could hear mom clip clopping down the hallway. When her footfalls stopped at the family room, Nana pulled you out of her shoulder bag and plopped you on the tray table. Then Nana looked at the lady and said, "OK Janice, tell her what you think."

I almost fell out of bed. Nana had showed my inner most thoughts to some strange lady who played bridge with stroke patients. Was she kidding me???

No. No she wasn't. The lady, Mrs. Mattingly, could see my concern. Concern? Heck. No. Not concern. And not anxiety. And not trepidation. I flipped out. Quietly of course. Nana looked at me and said, "Now calm down Genevieve. You look more horrified then you did when you first heard from a dead president. You know you can trust me. Mrs. Mattingly doesn't just play with any old cards. She has special cards." And then Mrs. Mattingly pulled a silk wrapped bundle from a giant can-vass tote bag. Inside the silk fabric, there were huge pieces of cardboard covered with painted pictures.

Still stunned, I said to Nana, "I've seen cards like those be-fore. I saw them at the fair. There was a lady with a booth, and she wore very colorful veils. She had lots of tattoos and rings all over her fingers and ears – earrings like BattyPatty – she looked so unusual. But Mrs. Mattingly looks like any other old lady." I glanced over at Mrs. Mattingly, "No offense."

"None taken," the polite seventy-something-year-old said. "I spent a few decades dressing the part too. Now I collect so-cial security and a small retirement my husband left me. I don't have to lure people in off the street to tell them their fortunes anymore. Now I can just focus on what I enjoy. Help-ing the living communicate with the dead."

I looked at Nana. I shook my head. I picked you up off the counter and flipped through you to make sure I hadn't lost any part of you while you were gone. Nope, even Mrs. Welch's notes survived the trip out with Nana. There they were. Still taped in place.

I spoke again, this time it was almost a whisper, "I'm the one on chemotherapy, but I think you guys have lost your marbles."

It was stone cold silent for a bit and then Nana explained, "Genevieve. I saw that you have a new message. I saw that Charlie Chaplin has taken the time to write to you. Although, after all Charlie had to say about Nat, I was a little disappointed that my favorite Jazz musician didn't comment more about himself."

(To tell the truth so was I).

Nana continued, "Be that as it may, what's important is, if I can see it, you are not hallucinating."

Yeah, and guess what Nana, Joe felt the heat in the room too. That's not a hallucination either, I thought. But I didn't interrupt her.

Nana went on: "Mrs. Mattingly is a medium. She communicates with other stages of life. After I read Charlie's letter to you, I thought, 'We need a professional. We need a psychic or a priest.' And well, Genevieve, I hate to admit it but, I didn't trust a priest not to have an agenda with a little chemo kid. I was afraid a priest would go for the God answer and never get to the bottom of what's going on with these dead guys. So, I went for the psychic first."

"So," I asked, "What we do now?" You know what they said? They told me they brought a deck of cards and they might tell me what was going on with my magic diary. I shook my head. I asked them how that might happen. And Mrs. Mattingly, taking no offense at my negative body language said, "We won't know until we see the cards."

I stared at Nana. Did she believe all this mumbo jumbo? I wanted to ask her, but I was the one holding a diary that had writing in it that was NOT DONE BY ME. At least not consciously done by me. Mrs. Mattingly explained that there could be something "supernatural" about my Tarot reading or it could be my subconscious mind telling me something part of me already knows. It was for me to decide which one was going on.

Nana was right, this was nothing like calling a priest. If a priest talks about spirituality, you know it's always supernatural. Let's face it, the purpose of God is to outmaneuver what's going on in nature.

Mrs. Mattingly had a nice face. She was average height and kinda skinny. She wore thick eyeglasses that made her eyes look too big. Her grey hair stuck out from the sides of a well-worn Boston Red Sox Baseball Cap. Little old ladies wearing baseball caps don't walk into your life every minute, so I asked her how long she'd been a fan. "How long have I loved the Red Sox?" She repeated my question only she changed the word I used "like" into the word she had for the team, "love."

Mrs. Mattingly continued, "I guess ever since I did a reading for Roger Clemens. Have you heard of him?"

I had.

I too love the Red Sox. Clemens? Not so much. Not since he left and played for the Yankees. The psychic went on to explain that Roger had gone to her early in his career, when he first started playing for the Red Sox. Mrs. Mattingly explained, "Roger and Deb – his wife – came to see me about the curse. You know, Babe Ruth's curse on the BoSox."

Many folks thought Babe Ruth who had been a clean straight arrow playing for the BoSox – as she called them – had cursed the team after they traded him to the New York Yankees. For years The Babe had played great for the Red Sox but became an alcoholic and a "lousy good for nothing womanizer" when he went to the Yankees, at least according to Nana. He played great ball for the New York team. In the end, his personal life fell apart and he died of – you guessed it – cancer. Throat cancer to be specific.

Nana always says, "He got cancer because of tobacco. At least he had a good reason for his."

I know one thing. There is no, underline no, reason for cancer: good or otherwise.

Anyway, Mrs. Mattingly went on, "You know, oh no you don't. How could you? I'm the psychic. Never mind, Roger tried to give me a Yankees hat a few Decembers ago. But I won't wear it. It was nice to see them though. See, Roger and Deb came for another reading. I hadn't seen either of them in years. The Baseball Hall of Fame was about to vote on who to induct in 2017. He had been high on the list early on and wanted to know if he would get in that time."

"Well," I asked, "What did you tell him?"

"I told him I didn't have a very good feeling about it. My psychic gut didn't think so," she said. "Then he muttered at me. I told him to speak up. I said I wouldn't waste my psychic powers figuring out what a timid ball player thought of me."

Nana and I looked at each other and chuckled at the thought of Mrs. Mattingly chewing out Roger Clemens.

Mrs. Mattingly continued, "You know what he told me when he piped up loud enough to be heard? He said, 'Mattingly, you paid too much attention to my indictment for lying to congress.' What an ego! He thought because congress had cleared him, found him not guilty of perjury, my sub-conscious still held the charges against him.

"I laughed and laughed. I asked him, if he had so little faith in my abilities, why did he continue paying for them? Then I reminded him, 'It's the conscious vote of others' that mattered, not my subconscious thoughts. But it's a good example of Tarot Card reading. Sometimes the cards tell you what you already know or think you know."

"So, it's not about communicating with the after-life or talking to the supernatural?" I asked.

Mrs. Mattingly said, "It's about all those things, for some people. Let's see what it's about for you. Shall we?"

Mrs. Mattingly explained that she kept the cards wrapped in silk, so they didn't pick up the vibes (my word, not hers. I forgot what she called it) of other people by accident. Mrs. Mattingly didn't want the cards telling me more about the lady in front of her in the grocery line that morning, than they did about me.

Mrs. Mattingly handed me the cards, her hand cradling them with the silk fabric between them and her skin. Then she told me to shuffle the cards, cut them and restack them three times.

Influence. That was the word. She didn't want the cards influenced by other people. I'm shaking my head while I write this all down. Influencing cards and then a piece of silk cloth being magic enough to keep them from being "influenced"! It's all as crazy as Nat King Cole thanking Charlie Chaplin for his kind words in my diary!

I gave her back the cards. She said she often drew 10 cards, but tonight she would draw four. I asked her why she would draw so few. And she told me she didn't know why. She didn't care why. Mrs. Mattingly *knew* she would only draw four.

Mrs. Mattingly put her hand on the deck and turned over the Princess of Hearts. She smiled and said pulling the Princess made her feel confident the reading would be about me. She had been afraid that since she had spent so much time talking to Nana, she might unintentionally have done a reading for her.

Mrs. Mattingly told me that the Princess of Hearts was either very emotional, or deeply concerned.

This was a reading? Couldn't the IV tubes and clumps of hair on my pajama shirt claim psychic powers then? Of course, this little princess is deeply concerned! So far not too impressed, Mrs. Mattingly.

The second card overturned showed a mature woman with a big gold coin in her lap. The paintings on the cards were so beautiful and detailed. Pieces of art.

Mrs. Mattingly explained that the Queen of Coins must be my mom. I protested, "What? Not Nana? Mom doesn't even know about this."

Mrs. Mattingly told me that mom's level of awareness didn't matter, because it was about me and I know mom. She told me "because the Queen was inverted." (She meant upside down) and that meant that things were all backwards for mom just now. Well, I agreed with her there. It wasn't Nana. Stuff was never topsy turvy for Nana. Mrs. Mattingly said this was about a woman who would – under other circumstances – be strong. But now all her strength seemed diminished by what was happening.

Still didn't seem to have any sixth sense. At least not to me. Anyone could see when they walked into the room earlier that mom had been crying really, really hard. We both had. Two for two for stating the obvious, Mrs. Mattingly.

Her third card scared the living tar out of me when she turned it over. There was a giant tower being struck by lightning. The tower had broken in two and people were falling out of the windows. Seriously, Mrs. Mattingly? Did that make sense? Show a card like that to a 14-year-old with cancer?

I looked at Nana. She played the mind reader this time and touched my hand as her eyes scrutinized the medium saying, "Mrs. Mattingly, that's not an appropriate card for this reading." Her tone kind of implied that she should have left a few of the more frightening cards out of the deck when she started.

Mrs. Mattingly replied, "No, it's not bad. Honest! The tower card doesn't stand for things being shattered, it stands for change. It doesn't signal death."

"Well death is change," I interrupted.

She agreed but said, "There are very definite cards for death. And this one encourages a person to be open to change." More importantly, she told me, I had to keep my eyes open for change. She said, "It's the same concept as seeing storm clouds parting."

Well a kid with cancer being told to brace herself for change. That didn't seem to earth shatteringly insightful either.

Then came the final card. The Magician!

Mrs. Mattingly looked from Me to Nana and back again and smiled. "Magic!" she exclaimed.

She looked so pleased. This card didn't appear by accident. Not in her mind.

I think the looks on our faces deflated her enthusiasm. So, her explanation took it down a notch.

"I know how you're feeling. I know that it feels like magic has been going on in that diary of yours, Genevieve," Mrs. Mattingly chimed, "but it could also mean a very wise person. A wise man.

"Or maybe a brilliant doctor?" This time it was Nana that

interrupted. "This place is full of wise men AND women."

"So that's the answer?" I asked. "Either there's magic going on, or I'm on a psychic collision course with a smart doctor? In a hospital of all places? Please forgive me for sounding like an obnoxious 14-year-old, but this doesn't feel very helpful considering I've got strange writing in my journal and I'm sick with cancer."

Mrs. Mattingly cooed at me, "Oh now you sound like Debra Clemens when I told her that her husband would leave the Boston Red Sox just like the Babe did and that he too would curse his former team.

"Look, Genevieve," she continued, "You think about what you've learned here. Think about your mom's strength being challenged. Think about change being upon you because the cards want you to think more about that. And then open your mind to the concept of magic, or..."

And her words trailed off. "Or what?"

(I'm sure she predicted I'd ask that!)

"Or that last card, the magician, could be a wise manipulator engaged in some sleight of hand to distract you."

Nana sighed. I think she had somehow hoped the reading would lead to something – I don't know – conclusive. Like what Nana? Some real information about dead correspondents? Seriously Nana?

Nana spoke, "So we're back where we started. It could just be someone playing tricks on Genevieve?"

Mrs. Mattingly smiled the sweetest smile I've ever seen. She placed her hand over my Nana's hand, and she said, "There is no evil in any of this. I promise. I feel nothing but goodness in this diary and in the messages from..."

"Beyond?" I blurted.

"From wherever, sweet skeptical Genevieve. Just relax and enjoy them. And I hope for everyone's sake you keep getting more contact from whatever the source of these messages is. Eventually and in all probability, that's how the mystery will be solved: with more contact."

Mrs. Mattingly wrapped her cards back in her silk cloth just as mom retuned to the room.

Everyone said goodbye and after my nighttime meds, I settled down to write this. It's a few minutes before midnight now and I'm pooped. Time for the excitement to end so I can go to sleep. But I'll be sleeping with a hope in my head. I hope I hear from someone new tonight.

No! Not you, Babe Ruth! No offense, Great Bambino, but I'd like to hear from a gentle soul. Maybe someone a little less complicated than a famous person with drug, alcohol and/or womanizing issues.

Sweet dreams, MD.

G ood Morning Miss Flynn,

It has come to my attention that you are in need of comfort. I am here, now, hoping to supply just that.

Forgive me for visiting you while you sleep. I have long held a reputation for moving through hospital wards at night. My purpose has always been to deliver relief from distress, and I have found patients and their surroundings often require extra attention at night. My contemporaries dubbed me "The Lady with the Lamp" because of these nocturnal wanderings.

Today, nursing schools all around the world use the symbol of a lamp in their literature. Institutions of higher learning have them manufactured in many varieties as tokens of appreciation for the work performed by those who toil in my vocation.

Indeed, I am gratified that such a place of honor has been set aside for the simple tool that illuminated darkened wards and hallways. That oil lamp guided me through my work with the ill and afflicted across time.

I am likewise gratified to be summoned to your bedside. Although, I must admit, it has been more than a century since my talents were put to any use at all.

I see that there has been quite some discussion of war in your daily record of events as they are presented here.

I have also noticed that you have named this record your *Magic Diary*. I assure you, I know nothing of magic and generally don't believe such a thing exists. But I **do** know that the second word comes from *dies*, the millennia old Latin word for *day*. Back in the 16th century, the Latin word *diarium* was employed to describe such a chronical. Later in England, they used the word, *diurnal*. Although **this daily** logbook was more often used to keep track of one's prayers.

The French gave us the word *jurnal* in the 14th century and it's still used today. Although your century had adapted the spelling. Journal likewise originates from *jour*, which is, of course, French for day.

Forgive me. I have taken us both off track. I would like to return to the topic of war.

I know you wanted a visitor who could be uplifting. But, as I think you beginning to understand, there is little good accomplished in our world that was not required because of a good deal of bad.

Allow me to digress and tell you something about myself. I was born in Italy to members of the British aristocracy. My family's wealth kept me from ever experiencing the cruel torment caused by poverty, overcrowding and malnutrition. Somehow, even though far removed, my mind obsessed about these scourges anyway.

My birth occurred just a few years after a great and terrible man abdicated his rule in neighboring France. You'll find as you study the course of human existence, that most individuals who attain great power have irredeemable qualities about their mortal soul. This was especially true of the Corsican Emperor of France, Napoléon Bonaparte.

Emperor Bonaparte's ego knew no bound. When he assumed power, he grabbed the crown from the hands of the pontiff and coroneted himself. Thereby illustrating that no ruler on earth was greater than he. Not even God's own representative, the pope!

In the emperor's youth, French hospitals were administered by the church. Indeed, prelates did all that could be done by most hospitals throughout history. Prayer was the single harmless treatment administered in these putrid places. Their regular prescriptions: bloodletting, leaches, and boils only made conditions worse. Doctors and surgeons delivered few cures – and then as a stroke of luck not genius. Most who could afford the most meagre of genuine medical assistance received these practitioners in their own home.

The Medical Arts were mysteries and contagious illnesses killed 95 out of every one hundred persons who had the misfortune to spend time in hospital.

Napoléon's controlling nature expanded far beyond the customary governing reach of the time. The emperor threw the churches out of the hospitals and administered them though the state. He demanded that information on all aspects of society be collected and evaluated. Statistics – the math of the state – told a tale of infection and contamination, not miasma or sin. But only those who observed the data firsthand bothered to learn that disease had a scientific origin, not a spiritual one.

Statistics gathering became as big an epidemic as cholera. The custom of accumulating scientific evidence swept through western Europe. Best practices – and worst practices – became evident. Many resisted new knowledge. Even your own President George Washington died because of the ignorance of his surgeons, not the illness upon him. Native Americans could have treated the president for the pneumonia he contracted. They would have soothed his symptoms with the help of herbs and roots they found in the forest. His strong body would have rallied to defeat his infection. Instead his doctors clung to their medieval medicine and bled him to death.

You see, Miss Flynn, some of us believe our eyes and change our habits for the betterment of the individuals in our care. Look how far medicine has come in your time! Look at what medical artists have done to mitigate suffering! I played a part in that change, and that is what I am here to tell you. I hope your spirits will be buoyed by what you learn.

When I was not much older than you, I approached my parents and told them I wanted to be a nurse. I felt a calling to change the world in a profound way. I felt convinced that I must join the nursing profession. Since this notion horrified my parents, my father forbade it.

"Nurses" of that time ranged in occupation from a child's handmaiden to a woman given to prostitution. Indeed, women who worked tending the sick often sold their bodies for sexual gratification to pay their bills. Debtor nurses, regardless of their noble desire to help others, would be put out and condemned to slog in the workhouses.

According to the census of Great Britain in 1851: 508 of the nation's nurses were between five and ten years of age. Another 7259 nurses were between the ages of 11 and 15. In the mid-19th century, child labor impacted society everywhere. Children were forced to toil as servants or labor in the workhouse. These working children had a meager life expectancy.

I noticed that Charlie Chaplin disclosed to you his own indentured past. He had been a pauper confined to toil in a workhouse. I'm grateful to the passage of time, because by the year Mr. Chaplin entered the poorhouse, my work cleaning them had made them a safer more hygienic experience. His labor remained drudgery of the meanest variety, but he needn't fear infectious outbreak the way he would have 50 years earlier.

As I grew into young adulthood, I turned down several offers of marriage. A young woman of means could better herself only by taking a suitable husband. I wanted nothing to do with that life of aristocratic tedium. I asserted my independence so completely that my father relented. I took a position in a local hospital for women.

That wasn't enough. My heart went out to my countrymen. I yearned to help the disadvantaged whom society had condemned to lamentable labour in houses designated for the poor. I used my elevated station to arrange tours of these facilities. The conditions in these workhouses rivaled and bested every squalor I had imagined. Most of the workhouse occupants were physically and mentally ill. The buildings overflowed with children who had been committed for the purpose of paying off debts incurred by their parents.

A legendary author you may know, Charles Dickens, famously wrote many essential novels exposing the cruel ugliness of poverty – most memorably – A Christmas Carol. Dickens detailed the lives of the abject poor impeccably: Not because he had a keen imagination, but because he had lived that way. Charles was first indentured at age 12 in one such ghastly place. He worked in a boot blacking factory to pay his father's debts. Miss Flynn, Charles story was as heartbreaking as it was ordinary. Despite Charles' years of child labor and sacrifice, the authorities remanded John Dickens to debtor's prison anyway. Time and again the elder Dickens creditors had him locked up.

In 1851, three years after his son published *A Christmas Carol*, John Dickens died of a bladder infection and ruptured urethra. John Dickens suffered in silence from these condition for years and I have no doubt that he contracted them during one of his many incarcerations.

Miss Flynn, I know from what you've written how nimble your mind is. I know you will understand what I am about to write. The wanton destruction of human life wounds us all. In my life this truth became my obsession. I had to do something. And I had many ideas about what could be done.

Because my parents held significant station in 19th century society, I had access to powerful Members of Parliament. I lobbied labour leaders to effect change. Workhouses had hospitals attached to them and the ill or incapacitated, whether physically unwell or by what you would call being "batty," would go there to convalesce or to die. Most died.

Many children with no training to care for the sick were confined to these squalid places, tending to the ill. Infectious disease and appalling sanitary conditions contributed to unforgivable mortality rates.

In the 1840's, no one understood how germs caused disease. No one even imagined that germs reproducing over and over in a human wound or vital organ could cause infection or the loss of life. The germ theory had not yet been invented by another awe-inspiring Frenchman, Louis Pasteur.

But many of us who worked daily with the unwashed victims of disease had our suspicions.

Over the years since Pasteur competed his work, scientists constructed methods incorporating the germ theory. One such surgeon, Sir Joseph Lister saved a seven-year-old boy's life by using an antiseptic before and while he operated on him in 1865.

Of course, senseless tragedy reigned for centuries before that time of discovery. Wars raged around the world, and countless soldiers died because their surgeons treated them in unsanitary conditions without the benefit of modern scientific advances like Lister's antisepsis. In civilian life, filth and ignorance killed huge swaths of the population. Disease spread. Infections choked the life out of mothers after child-birth.

Within a decade, my reputation as an activist, outspoken advocate, and champion against child labour had reached the highest levels of government. My reputation for nursing and my nursing practices secured me a job working in one of those earlier wars: One of the myriad wars before the invention of antisepsis.

The changes I made mattered because war matters. War has value to rulers. Soldiers – disposable peasants at peace time – have value in war.

Mind you, my work saving the lives of incarcerated debtors provided little financial reward to the kingdom. You see, Miss Flynn, paupers were easily replaced. Saving soldiers, expensively trained, outfitted and repositioned to war zones, made solid financial sense.

Miss Flynn, I'm sorry to take so much room in your diurnal. You asked for something uplifting, and I hope to have you awaken to a new understanding of the magnificent lengths to which your nurses and their assistants go on your behalf. Even the person who comes to your room to wash your toilet basin assists in your recovery from this awful disease which afflicts you. Some medicine is curative, some is palliative, but none functions well without the ongoing preventative measures taken by the nursing and housekeeping staff.

Also, it's been quite a long time since I've written anything. Even though my *Notes on Nursing* published by Harrison, *Bookseller to the Queen,* is still referenced in nursing schools today. I suppose I'm indulging myself a fair ration, here, by writing so much.

Lastly, I hope this lends still more perspective to the role war plays in the overall picture of humanity. As I mentioned, war has value to those who wage it. That is why it has become the breeding ground of innovation.

On the 4th of November 1854, I and 38 nurses arrived in a city then called Constantinople. Today you call it Istanbul, in the nation of Turkey. Her Majesty's Minister of War, Baron Sidney Herbert, had called me to the Crimean War where battle raged between Britain, Russia, and their allies, for two bloody, disease-drenched years.

Because of my work with the poorhouses and hospitals back home in London – I was asked to save the lives of our soldiers who had survived a battle only long enough to die in hospital.

Scutari, the British military hospital to which I was assigned, had a mortality rate greater than 70 percent when I arrived. I had seen many atrocious things in the poorhouse hospitals, but my nurses and I could not have imagined the horrors that awaited us by the battlefield.

The wounded were lying in excrement. Body fluids of every kind lay on their mattresses and flooded the floors around their beds. The hospital itself had been built above a cesspool filled with human waste. Rats, insects and other vermin infested the living quarters of the injured and the dying. Soap, bandages, and clean water had to be rationed because our scant supplies were inadequate to the task.

With only 38 nurses I didn't have enough help to bring the hospital up to my sanitary standards. If the wounded were at all healthy, I put them to work cleaning beside us.

I created a laundry service so that the beds had clean linens. I didn't just clean where the soldiers were treated and slept. I removed the refuse and disposed of it as far away from the hospital as possible. We didn't have the germ theory yet, but common sense demanded cleanliness. And yes, Pasteur's science would later support this hypothesis.

I had a fundamental understanding of nutrition. I improved the food and kitchen facilities. I knew malnourished patients could not recover.

Nutrition is something I encourage you to remember, Miss Flynn. I'm sure you remember from your last exposure to chemotherapy that the side effects include extreme nausea. Remember, wasting is a major concern for chemotherapy patients. I understand many of your hospitals are now allowed to prescribe cannabis to improve these lost appetites. There is also synthetic THC, although it is not believed to work as well as the original compound in its organic form. Either one, however, will improve your appetite and relieve your nausea. And they don't smell bad like those enormous gray pills the doctors expected you to take as a young child. I know that choking them down often caused vomiting episodes all by themselves.

Back to Crimea.

Under my direction, the mortality rate at Scutari dropped from three fourths of all patients to fewer than one in twenty. Prior to my nurses and I taking control of the facility, infectious diseases had killed far more soldiers than did their battle wounds. We eliminated most of the infections and the corresponding mortality.

After a year and a half, I returned home and wrote an 830-page report entitled, *Notes on Matters Affecting the Health, Efficiency and Hospital Administration of the British Army.* Queen Victoria honored me as nobility would expect to be honored, with jewels and praise.

And for a while, the medical community listened.

I built a nursing school and trained others who went on to build more.

The great American Nurse, Clara Barton, learned our techniques and worked with others in the United States of America as they struggled to save lives sacrificed in the great tragedy of your Civil War. As I'm sure you know, Clara went on and founded the American Red Cross. The number of lives she saved is as enormous as it is unknowable.

But politics and science are not often good friends. Many politicians worked with practitioners that denied the gains Pasteur, Lister, myself and others had made in the medical arts – what are now referred to as health sciences. They attacked our findings. They denied my work.

Miss Flynn, I assure you, I hadn't cleaned out a hospital built on a cesspool to be dissuaded by some steaming cistern of rebuke in Parliament.

I continued speaking in favor of good food, personal hygiene, hospital cleanliness and comfort for the afflicted. I insisted that nurses be educated and wrote the curriculum myself. Curriculum still used today in the education of your very own nursing staff.

I'm grateful for the upper-class upbringing that without doubt contributed to the unrelenting nature of my character and my bravery in the face of powerful opposition. Had I been born to a poor family, I never could have spoken out. I'm grateful for the wisdom instilled in me by my creator. I'm grateful for my shared experiences with the poor and the afflicted. Because of my many gifts – the ones born into me and the ones acquired in life – my educated guesses proved invaluable. My thoughts on nursing were correct before my contemporaries had the scientific explanations to support me and my assertions.

What does all this mean? It means... Be brave, Miss Flynn. Don't question what you already know in your heart to be true. I'm not saying you should be unyielding to every new concept that comes into your head. But don't be closed minded or too attached to old ways of thinking either.

Please don't be like the wooden headed doctors of the 17th, 18th, and 19th centuries who insisted that bleeding a patient was the best way to get rid of an illness: all the while remaining oblivious to the infections they carried from patient to patient on their own bloody surgical gowns.

Germs were invisible to the surgeons of the 18th century, just as I am invisible to you. You can't explain my presence. Neither can your grandmother. But don't deny the better feeling you have now that you know I exist. Remember, I didn't just help people by cleaning their linens. I also comforted their hearts and the hearts of their loved ones. I wrote letters to the families of fallen soldiers. I'm convinced those letters were every bit as important a part of my medicine as the time I spent scrubbing the floors beneath their beds.

May you have a comforted heart and a healed body, Miss Flynn.

Sincerely Yours,
Nightingale

Florence Nightingale?

Really, MD?

Is she even real? I never thought she was real. I mean with a name like Nightingale, I just assumed that somebody invented her. Like Luna the Tick sidekick. Nightingale, Lunatic. I mean, I think I even thought about her when I was making Luna up. Or BattyPatty. They all sound just as crazy, just as fake.

Still, I'm glad she came to visit me. I knew someone had been here as soon as I opened my eyes in this stifling room. And it wasn't the Sultan of Swat, the Big Bam. Glad of that, too.

Hey, I got some nerve. Getting picky about which dead legend comes to visit and write in my diary.

But, like Nana said yesterday, when she and I were speculating about who might come visit next: She said if I were going to hear from some famous dead ball player, she'd rather have it be Jackie Robinson. Old 42. The black man who broke the color barrier. Nana told the psychic lady yesterday, "I wouldn't worry about Roger Clemens getting hung up for his drug use." Nana put her hands on her hips and continued, "Babe Ruth never played against a black man. That's the kind of cheating that hurts more than a ball game. It hurts society too." I think she's right. You can't call Babe's record clean either.

Anyway, so Florence Nightingale comes instead of the late great – and not so great – ball players. Why? To tell me what? I mean, she was incredulous that humanity values war over what?

All else?

Sure, seems that way. The worlds' leaders would justify killing villagers or soldiers by telling people war helps them protect what we all value. Liberty or the homeland. But wouldn't those things be better defended with goodness? Kindness? Generosity from the wealthy powers to the poor powers?

Oh yeah, and Nightingale (that's how she signed her letter) wanted me to know something else. Ready for this? She wanted me to try marijuana! Wow. Now that's what I call a consultation! MD, I'm shaking my head here. What do I do when the nutritionist comes in today to make recommendations?

"Hi, did you ever learn about Florence Nightingale in college? Oh, you did? She was an important part of modern nursing and dietary medical support? You don't say. Well... what do you think she'd think of cannabis? Oh, and do you think you could score me a couple of joints and we'll find out how it works on my nausea?"

Mmm. I think they sell it for medical use in the next state over. I wonder what kind of trouble you could get into by bringing it across state lines. "Hey officer dude. Yeah, this bag is for my little buddy on the eighth floor. Dude! **Seriously.** Dude! I'm taking it to a kid with cancer."

On go the handcuffs. Kazzu, you ready to run another jury?

Nightingale called it though. I've lost my appetite. And if I start puking, I won't want that appetite back. Maybe I'll ask Joe what he's heard about marijuana when I see him tomorrow for physical therapy. I'm sure he has a few ideas of how it works on nausea and he's a cool guy. He won't goof on me too bad for asking.

"Hey kid. Why do you think they call it dope, anyway?"

I opened the window. It's cooling off in here, finally! I wonder what time it is. I wonder where everyone is. I could ring for the nurse. But I don't need to see anyone.

I mean come on, I've had the founder of modern nursing in here giving me advice tonight, that'd be a hard act to follow.

Besides, I don't want to "cry wolf" too often. That's what Nana calls it when you trick someone into paying attention to you. Nope, no wolves in here: A few disembodied historical figures, but no wolves.

I never knew that about Clara Barton. She learned nursing at one of the Nightingale schools and went on to her own greatness. I mean the Red Cross is everywhere now.

One time I shared a room with a little kid who'd been in a bad car accident. He had been climbing down out of his school bus and a car didn't stop even though the lights had been flashing on the back of the bus. Nana said she heard that the guy had been texting and hadn't noticed the flashers were on.

"Can't fix stupid," Nana says. She said they should just take his license away for good cause they "Can't fix stupid."

So anyway, this little kid had a ruptured spleen and he'd shattered both his arm and leg. All the junk he got messed up and broken were along the same side of his body, but I can't remember which side right now. I'll have to look up where to find the spleen when mom brings back her iPad.

Anyway, all of a sudden, this army guy comes walking in the room with camouflage clothes and a big backpack.

This kid who shouldn't have moved – at all – darn near jumps out of his bed 'cause he's so happy to see the guy. Turned out the soldier was his dad. He'd been deployed a few months earlier to one of those awful wars in the middle east. Iraq or Afghanistan.

I can't remember that any better than I can remember the side he busted up in the accident.

Jonas, that was his name. The kid's name was Jonas.
Anyway, Jonas asked his dad how he'd gotten to come home. The dad told him that the Red Cross had done it. Jonas mom had called the Red Cross and they had worked with the army to bring the dad home.

Nice work Clara Barton. Nice work Jonas' mom. Nice work Nightingale. That's some crazy connectivity.

I'm glad I remembered Jonas and his dad. I'm glad I got to watch them see each other for the first time since Jonas' accident. Some days it sure feels like I've gotten more good from this stupid cancer than I've gotten bad. That little fact might've held true if I hadn't relapsed. The relapse could be a deal breaker.

But in the meantime, I'll just be grateful for some of it. Most kids never get to see some of the great things I've seen.

Nice memory, Nightingale. Thanks for the visit.

Hi Genevieve,

Thanks for the shout out to black athletes. I'm not here to say anything negative about Babe Ruth or Roger Clemens, or any other white competitor. I guess when you've beaten as many white athletes as I have, you come to respect the enormous amount of effort it takes to get to first place – regardless of racism. And you sure don't get to number one, in my sport, without being tested by white guys with lots of talent, determination and strength. Trust me. Those white athletes I played against; they were tough!

Did you ever hear of Jimmy Connors? Well, I beat him, and that victory impressed me more than it did anyone. Beating Jimmy made me the greatest tennis player in the world. Not just the best black player (not much of an accomplishment because there were only a handful of us) but the best player regardless of race.

Besides, becoming the greatest tennis player of my lifetime wasn't the greatest challenge I ever faced. It wasn't even the greatest accomplishment.

Still, I never could've become world champion if others hadn't sacrificed for me and believed in me.

See, Genevieve, black men – and women – have to stand up against a lot of odds before they ever get into the ring, or onto the field, or dive in a pool, or step out on the court.

My whole life story is different from other black pros because of the sport that attracted me. I didn't have to excel in a black league like Jackie Robinson. Because nobody pushed enough tennis in black neighborhoods, we never ended up with a segregated sport. Nope, one day I walked onto the court of white athleticism and stunned them.

Did you ever hear of Robert Frost? Robert Frost was a poet. He was poet laureate for the United States back in John Kennedy's administration. One of his poems went like this:

"I shall be telling this with a sigh
Somewhere ages and ages hence:

Two roads diverged in a wood, and I
— I took the one less traveled by,
And that has made all the difference."

Genevieve, that road less traveled by, it sure made all the difference in my life. Let me tell you a little about that road.

I was born in the segregated south back in 1943. My mom, dad and my kid brother lived in Richmond, Virginia. My mom died when I was little, just six years old. My brother, was five years younger. Our dad worried that two little black boys might get in trouble, so he watched over us every minute of every day.

Our dad worked hard, and he cared about others. He taught us to care about others too.

Our dad worked the **kind of jobs** black men could get in those days. He chauffeured wealthy folks around and one of those fat cats got him a job as a security guard at the park where I went to play.

From the moment I picked up a tennis racket, it felt right in my hand. Lucky for me, some great coaches and players noticed I could play. I got scholarships and offers to play on prestigious teams. Ever hear of the Davis Cup? Well, I won't go into all that here. Suffice to say in 1965, I became the first African American to win the NCAA singles crown.

But the Vietnam War had started by then. I enlisted in the Army reserves so I could finish college. When I graduated from UCLA, my kid brother had just finished up a tour in Vietnam. The U.S. government had a rule back then. No two brothers could be in combat at the same time. My brother, Johnnie, re-enlisted and went back to Vietnam so they wouldn't take me. So, I could keep on playing tennis.

Genevieve, more than any other person who helped me in my career, my brother Johnnie sacrificed to make sure I'd become the man history needed me to be.

Being a star athlete changed my life in a way that no other force could have. I **made history**. I **shattered stereotypes**. I broke records. I fought apartheid.

Genevieve, by now you've noticed that famous people have

a spotlight that follows them around. If the best tennis player in the world gets a visa for South Africa and plays in the South African open, the world notices. If that man is black, the world gasps with fright or delight – depending on the observer.

See, in 1973 South Africa maintained a policy they called Apartheid. It mirrored our own segregation but with a touch of slavery thrown in too. Nobody much cared when blacks were killed or disappeared. Black African civil rights leaders got locked up and the South African Government threw away the key.

Unlike the United States, South Africa's ruling white people were the minority race. Afraid of the consequences of their domination, whites maintained control with murderous oppression tactics employed to stifle dissent among the black majority. As in the American Jim Crow deep south, blacks were slaughtered for speaking out. But in the late 20th century, what had been a river of murder and shame in the U.S. was a torrent in South Africa. When I first tried to play in the South African Open, the authorities stopped me. I was denied a visa three times before the South African government allowed me to enter their country. I played the whitest sport in THE white supremacist country, and along with my white doubles partner, Tom Okker, from the Netherlands, I won.

I see you studied World War II in school this year. Perhaps your history books told you about Jesse Owens who stunned a gape-jawed Adolf Hitler by winning four Olympic gold medals in Germany. But Genevieve, there were 18 blacks on that team. Owens is the only name anyone has remembered. That's how history remembers minorities who change the world. As loners.

As my brother Johnnie's sacrifice points out, nothing could be further from the truth.

Even more erased from history than the many blacks who competed in the 1936 Olympics, Genevieve, were the U.S. Jews in the competition. The two Jewish athletes sent by the U.S. to those Berlin games weren't allowed to compete at all. No one ever talks about them. They were denied their Olympic dream because the U.S. Olympic Committee Chairman, Avery

Brundage, didn't want to embarrass Hitler when the Jews won Gold Medals.

I know, Brundage displayed a despicable lack of courage.

But I want you to know that the famous one, the one black man that got all the attention. He didn't waste his spotlight. That's right. Jesse Owens spoke up for Marty Glickman and Sam Stoller. He offered his place in the relay so that one of them could win a gold. That is what great men do with their celebrity. And weak men that history will rightfully forget, like Avery Brundage, often make what little name they have by trampling on the greatness of others.

We all know the unfortunate outcome of a world willing to tolerate Hitler.

In my time, the South African persecution of blacks harkened back to that evil.

When I got my spotlight, I had to find a way to defeat white athletes in a segregated nation. I had to prove my fundamental equality to prove the fundamental equality of all people of color.

As for my personal stand against Apartheid? No, it sure didn't feel like I changed anything at all. Apartheid lived on, long past my exhibition of black equality back in 1973. The agony of segregation, subjugation, and exploitation along with the continued incarceration of South African civil rights leaders slogged on until 1994. In fact, Genevieve, I never saw it end. The year before the white government fell, I died of pneumonia caused by the Acquired Immune Deficiency Syndrome known as AIDS.

Here's something I want you to take to heart, Genevieve. Long debilitating illnesses complicate our lives, but they don't have to stop us from being great. We can triumph in spite of them.

As for me, my health care challenges began in 1979 when I had a heart attack that ended my career playing tennis. A blood transfusion during a coronary bypass surgery infected me with the Human Immunodeficiency Virus (HIV) and that, in turn, caused a brain tumor. During the surgery to remove the tumor the doctors discovered that I had the underlying

HIV infection.

But I still had a lot to do.

I went on to champion the cause of Haitian refugees when the United States deported them and repatriated them. Because I was rich and famous, and I didn't have to care if my skin – like theirs – was black, when my government arrested me at a protest in 1992, they immediately set me free. I stunned the media when I spoke out for other people of color who suffered without a voice. Politicians and my peers noticed my actions. *Sports Illustrated* magazine named me "Sportsman of the Year."

I spoke about human rights to everyone who would hear me. I worked as hard for inner city kids in the U.S. as I did for kids from Haiti or South Africa. I started health programs and youth organizations. I hoped to discover other young tennis greats in a community where no one else bothered to look. Serena and Vanessa Williams first played tennis in one of my programs. If you don't know who they are, look them up. You'll be impressed.

Boy, I feel like I'm just bragging about my life to you, Genevieve. It would be hard not to boast, with all the good fortune I've had. But I don't want you to think I'm unique.

I'm only one of so many excellent African Americans: athletes or otherwise. If this letter piques your interest, read my book, *Hard Road to Glory: A History of the African American Athlete.* Our struggle and triumph makes for an amazing tale I think you may find fascinating.

One last thing, Genevieve. As my comments about Glickman and Stoller imply, many minorities suffered oppression. Many minority athletes inspired their people and cried out for social justice when the white power structure considered them spectacles rather than role models. To make that point, I invited the man that 20th century sports writers named the best athlete of their century to contact you. Perhaps you've heard of him. He's accepted my invitation and has joined me here to write to you next.

Warmest wishes,

Arthur Ashe

Thank you, Arthur.

The best athlete of the 20th century? That's quite an honor. And all this time I thought having a small town in Pennsylvania coal country named after me was the most outlandish tribute I could receive.

Hello Genny. I'm sure you enjoyed your visit from Arthur. Such a good and decent man. In his time, he reminded us, "True heroism is remarkably sober, very undramatic. It is not the urge to surpass all others at whatever cost, but the urge to serve others at whatever cost."

I don't know what Arthur wanted me to tell you. Except maybe: don't give up. But I don't think I need to, you seem like quite a fighter. I admire your stamina. I had a lot of drive, but even I got bogged down in the heavy weeds that swallowed up Babe Ruth and so many other great athletes.

It's different though, for white men. Babe's alcoholism wasn't blamed on his race, but mine was. Prejudice leads many to believe that Native Americans drink too much because we have a defect. Bigots explain it away, not as an insidious plan by whites to control Indians, but as a part of our destructive make up. No one ever said, "Babe resorted to drinking because his whiteness made him inferior."

Don't get me wrong, I don't blame bigots for my shortcomings. But, bear that in mind when I give them no credit for my great achievements either.

I came from an Oklahoma reservation. I am a member of the Sac and Fox nation. Both my parents died and according to the custom of the day, I got shipped off to an Indian school and away from my people. I ended up in south central Pennsylvania.

They designed the Carlisle Concentration Camp (that's what it was, even though they called it the Carlisle Indian Industrial School) to deprive native children of their heritage. Today the old campus is part of the U.S. Army War College. But the graveyard remains. Buried there are scores of little children who died from abuse or homesickness or disease or broken hearts: or all the above.

I fared better than most of my Indian classmates because I

excelled at sports. No, not just one sport, every sport. Like Jesse Owens, I went on to win Olympic gold medals. The pentathlon and decathlon require an athlete to compete in a wide range of events. So, to win the gold in both, as your math teacher, Mr. Murray, would tell you, I had to master 15 events in total.

On the second day of the competitions, which required running and jumping along with throwing and other skills, my shoes were stolen. With no other option before me, the coach pulled two mismatched shoes from the trash and I won the contests roughshod. Mind you, only one of the shoes fit. What they didn't understand about me was that, as a native, I hadn't relied on clothing to master any of my talents. In fact, when the track coach discovered me in high school, I was performing the high jump. I was 5'9" tall and I jumped a 5'8" high bar wearing a pair of coveralls - the kind you see on farmers.

Because I'd never had much, I didn't expect much. I could get by with even less.

Here's something you might find it interesting: the first pentathlon and decathlon team featured a guy named Avery Brundage. You remember him, Genny, he was the Olympic Commissioner who chose Hitler's feelings over the hopes and dreams of those two Jewish athletes. That's what civil rights historians call a very interesting coincidence. No, of course I'm not saying he's the one who stole my shoes. But he sure as heck would have benefitted if I had not performed well.

Never mind that. I won.

King Gustav V of Sweden proclaimed me the finest athlete in the world.

The celebrations were short lived, the Olympic committee took that title away from me. They stripped me of my medals. You see, Genny, two years before I won the gold, I had played farm league baseball for hire. They disqualified me. They called me an "ineligible professional athlete."

Native Americans know disappointment. I moved on. I played professional football, baseball and basketball. Advertisers put my likeness on the cover of cereal boxes (in the photo they used my picture wearing a Canton jersey. It had a big C on it: for Canton. But no matter how many different 'C's I wore. They all still reminded me of the Concentration Camp where Indian kids were supposed to forget their culture and heritage, their language and families).

Some folks embraced my athleticism as heroism. Schools were named after me. These folks admired me.

Other people despised me. The even called me a "lazy Indian." They said I didn't work for my "gifts." They thought dumb luck had blessed me with a 185 lb. physique that was – for the most part – muscle. I had a 42-inch chest, 32-inch waist, and 24- inch thighs. These people were wrong. Maybe jealousy clouded their judgement. More likely, prejudice corrupted their minds. I worked hard to be strong. I ran with my dogs and they never lost me. Even though I was poor, I kept my protein intake up. I ate fried squirrel for breakfast.

From the outside looking in at Jim Thorpe, from most historical perspectives, my life looks like it ended in tragedy. I had three wives and eight kids. Even though I acted in the movies, often portraying an Indian, I was seldom respected as a performer. At the end of my life I worked for construction companies or did various other menial tasks. I was flat broke by the 1950's and when I got lip cancer, I had to get mercy care.

When I was on top of the world, I had one hell of a good time. When I fell, I laid low. I died too young. And I never got my medals back. Not while I was alive, anyway.

Lots of folks worked to turn history's recollection of me. Even former President Gerry Ford. (Now that's a good guy, Genny, I hope he visits you). Ford had played professional football. He understood how they'd robbed me and my family. At long last, in 1982, the Olympic Committee gave those gold medals back. Well, they returned them under certain conditions. But isn't that how everything gets returned when the offending parties would have to admit guilt otherwise?

Genny, I was one famous Indian in an era when most of my people weren't even considered Americans. Just like Arthur said, I don't begrudge any white athlete that did or didn't want to compete against me. Well, maybe one. The one who stole my shoes.

Get better Genny. This is your Olympics. I know you can get your gold! With my sincere affection to your mom and your grand mom,

I am,

Jim Thorpe

What the heck, Nana!!!!

What was she thinking bringing Roger here? Oh, never mind. I don't even want to think what she might have been thinking.

I opened my eyes, and leaning over my face, feeling the lymph glands on either side of my neck was Dr. Borlasa. "Trying to sweat the cancer out, are you, Genevieve?" she said. She smiled and crooked her head back to look at Nana AND WHEN SHE DID, I saw Roger standing over against the wall.

My eyes must've jumped out of my face. Nana acted like she hadn't noticed my shocked look turn into a dirty look and says, "Yeah, Genevieve, why on earth did you turn the thermostat up so high? Do you have chills?" And then she WINKS AT ME!

Oh, Nana. That wink doesn't work for you every time and this wasn't even one of those times when it kind of didn't work. No Nana, this time it didn't work at all.

Dr. Borlasa, shrewd medical professional that she is, does notice the glare I'm giving Nana and figures out I might be a little horrified to see Roger in the room. So, she asks, "Oh, could we get a little privacy in here? This will only take a minute." So, Nana huffs a little and takes Roger by the arm and leads him out to the hallway.

"Better?" Dr. Borlasa asked. "Much," I croaked.

Dr. Borlasa asked me the usual questions. How am I feeling? How's my new port? (That's how the medicine gets into my body). Have I got any rashes? How's the food? Then she starts on the unusual questions. Any more hallucinations? Room hot enough for ya? Who is Roger?

I was grateful that she asked about Roger. Not that I wanted to talk about the smartest boy in my school. The boy I've never seen OUTSIDE SCHOOL BEFORE! But I didn't want to talk about the hallucinations, the dead people, their intriguing words of wisdom and comfort, and ummm, AND the FIRES OF HELL belching forth, heating my room whenever someone wrote in my – oh yeah Dr. Borlasa – didn't I mention – MAGIC DIARY! Did I share with you the little fact that I'm the only one writing in it that isn't dead – YET!

It's so hot. I know I have more messages. But I haven't had time to look. I've been too busy telling my doctor that for some PHENOMENALLY insane reason, my grandmother ran into Roger Levinson at the grocery store and when he asked how I was doing – which he only asked – TO BE POLITE – Nana responded like a deranged psychopath and said, "I'm going there now. Why don't you come see for yourself?"

I don't need cancer to kill me. I'm getting the electric chair when I strangle my grandmother.

So yeah, half my hair is gone, and I puked about three times today. So, everything's normal, Doc. Except for the part where my grandmother brings in the smartest boy, cutest too, that I've ever met... to see me in the hospital. Which she shouldn't have done, but if she couldn't control herself, she could have gotten me a hat! I could have taken a shower. They have showers on the 8th floor you know, Nana!

Oh yeah, and the hallucinations are all gone. Nothing to worry about there, Doc. I mean, you can feel how hot it is yourself. Joe felt it too. **And the psychic. And mom. And the nurse. And Nana. And now** at least three of us can see the entries in my diary. Except me, I haven't seen the new ones because my panic attack hasn't ended yet.

Thank you, Mrs. Welch, for giving me this journal, or I'm pretty sure I would have passed out by now. The fear of having it discovered is the only thing keeping me from dying of - what do you professionals call it? - Teen angst!

So anyway, Dr. Borlasa leaves. I smooth my hair down the best I can. Nana and Roger come back in the room. Just for a minute because Nana tells me she must run another errand. She sends a text for Alma to pick her up and skedaddles out of the room (as she calls it) and on her way turns to Roger and says, "I'll only be about an hour. Why don't you have a nice visit and I'll be back to give you a ride home."

You know she didn't wink at me on her way out because I would have jumped from this bed, IVs and all, and poked that winking eye right out of her head!

Roger sat down and shifted a little in his chair. He said, "How's it going?"

I said, "Fine."

We stared at each other for like, 16 hours and then he said, "What's that?" He was pointing right at you, MD.

I told him you were just a notebook that Mrs. Welch gave me to keep track of my experiences.

Roger said, "Wow, it looks like you've had it for a long time. It looks like the whole thing is filled up with writing."

I wanted to say, "Helps when other people do most of the writing for you." But I didn't. I said, "Yeah. It helps me process my thoughts. I spend a lot of time alone in here. I think that must be why my grandmother kidnapped you and brought you here. I'm so sorry she did that to you."

You know what Roger said? It near about stopped my already chemo-laden overtaxed heart. He said, "I'm not."

He looked straight at me and said, "I'm not."

I looked down. I slid my hand over top of you and pulled you onto my lap. Like holding you might protect me or something. The temperature of my cheeks surpassed the hotness of the room.

"Wow, it's super hot in here," I whispered.

Roger replied, "It's a lot better than when I first walked in." Then he continued, in a voice so sweet, "I think I might have embarrassed you. I'm sorry. I thought you knew how I felt. I mean, I always say 'hi' to you at school. And there was that time I sent you the valentine."

I shot a glance up at him. "That was you?" I asked. "Last year? The one with the moving truck on it that said, 'You Move Me.'"

"Yeah," he said, "it was the least corny one I could find. You don't strike me as the kittens or teddy bears type."

The smartest boy in the school strikes again.

Then he confessed, "When you didn't say anything about getting it? I thought I embarrassed you. Or that you just didn't like me. So, it surprised me when your grandmother invited me to visit you."

I couldn't believe my ears. I blurted out, "You numbskull, there was no signature in the card."

Roger stared at me wide-eyed for a few minutes and then

"crack" he slapped himself in the forehead. He hit himself so hard the sound made me jump. Then he let his head fall into his lap. He was still clutching his forehead when I heard a muffled comment, "I forgot to sign the card. How could I have forgotten to sign the card?"

Then he pulled his head back up and looked straight at me and said, "What did you call me? Did you call me a numb-skull?"

We both busted up laughing.

We laughed and laughed. And after that everything seemed – well – it seemed: OK.

We spoke about school and he caught me up on things I had missed. Like Phillip Pyles winning the state title in the Lincoln-Douglas debates: as a freshman! Roger might be the smartest guy in the school, but we all know Phillip has – hands down – the best intellect mixed with verbal skills. He's used them to our advantage on more than one occasion.

For example, Phillip talked our principal into letting us watch the 1982 horror film classic, *The Swamp Thing*. "Because," he said, "it would help us understand the emotional instability of high school students." The principal – no lie – called an assembly and let Phillip get up and tell everyone that the film represented how we all feel when we're growing up, going through puberty, and how tough it is just to get up in the morning. One day, out of nowhere, we look in the mirror and see a pimple faced monster staring back at us. We don't know where our sweet childlike faces went... or if we'll ever get them back. It was sheer genius.

I liked that Roger admired Phillip. You've got to love a smart guy smart enough to know that other smart guys aren't a threat to them.

We ended up having a nice visit. By the time Nana returned to take Roger home, he had already asked if he could come back. I told him I'd like to see him again, but I couldn't be sure how long I'd be in the hospital. I'd already stayed three days and I shouldn't be in any more than eight or nine.

I explained to him, "They'll keep me on chemo long past the time I spend in the hospital. Once they get me stable, I'll be able to finish up my treatments as an outpatient."

He smiled and said, "It'll be nice to have you back at school."

I know, sweet, right?

We agreed to play it by ear. And then, I did something I never would have dreamed of doing an hour earlier. I gave him Nana's cell phone number. I said, "You can call her, and she can keep you posted. I'm sure she'll bring you back if I'm still here. And you still want to come."

"Otherwise," I repeated his well wishes, "I'll see you at school."

He smiled the dreamiest smile at me and headed out the door.

When Nana came back from dropping Roger off at his house, she asked if I'd had a nice visit. I told her I had several of them!

I let her read all the new interesting entries that had been posted here. She surprised me when she started crying reading about Jim Thorpe. Nana's borne a nasty grudge about the lousy treatment colonists gave the native people. She says it "irks" her that white men refuse to stop. Let me tell you, when Nana's irked, that means she's ready to blow.

"That bit about stealing his shoes takes the cake," Nana grumbled. "I bet it was that jerk who went on to pander to Hitler." She emphasized "was" when she said it. Nana continued, "We're still messing with the Indians. They are trying to protect their water out in North Dakota from the oil pipeline. People act like it's still 1850 and they are the railroad barons. Wealthy companies and individuals used the U.S. Army to steal the land from the Indians then, and they're using the sheriff's department and FBI to do it now."

Nana continued her running commentary. I didn't say much. When Nana fumes about things, it's best to let her be. Besides, I was tired and had a lot of homework.

After I finished my algebra assignment. We relaxed and sat still for a while. Until mom came back in. Then Nana sprung back to life. She looked over at mom and asked her, "Did you know your daughter has a crush on a boy named Roger Levinson?"

Oh man, there was blood everywhere. I couldn't believe it. I got up to go to the bathroom, I got my foot caught on the IV stand and boom! Down I went. I can't believe I did that. I grabbed for my bed's tray table and it slid away from me, too. Then I bashed my face into the side of the bed. I cut my cheek and bonked my nose a good one. And then – gush – blood! Everywhere!

Worst thing of all was that Mom had propped her feet up on my bed and she had fallen asleep in the chair. When I went crashing to the floor, she jolted herself awake and somehow caught herself before she too, landed on the floor, right across from me on the other side.

It was dark. So, before Mom could see me, she kept calling my name. I wanted to cry, the pain shot through my cheek. I thought my head might explode. I wanted to shout. I wanted to tell Mom to stop calling me. I wanted to do something. But I couldn't catch my breath. Mom came whipping around the bed and saw me there, on all fours, blood pouring from my nose and cheek and then she lost it. Mom went ballistic, hollering things and shouting for the nurse.

It sounded – and looked – like someone was getting murdered in the room.

One of the charge nurses flew in the doorway and flicked the lights on. Even in all that chaos, it made me think of Nightingale and her evening shifts caring for the sick. She'd have been proud of nurse Jane tonight. Jane sure didn't waste any time getting in to help us. And she must be way stronger than she looks. She had me up off that floor, on top of the bed, in a single motion. She grabbed towels from the bathroom and handed them to me.

Then – and yeah, it always goes this way – she stepped away from me and checked on Mom. "Are you OK, Mrs. Flynn?"

Mom assured her she'd be alright. Although none of us believed her. She apologized for freaking out. Still stammering and sputtering she tried to explain, "It, it, it was just that I got startled. In an instant I went from asleep to awake." Then she went on about how horrible it was to see all that blood.

With Mom calming down and me pressing once-white towels to my face, Jane came back over and took a better look at what I'd done to myself.

Jane knew what we all know, but she told it to us anyway, "That chemo you're on damages the clotting mechanisms in your blood. Not only did you get a nasty gash, your blood is flowing better than it is supposed to under normal healthy conditions."

Jane cleaned up my face while she continued explaining in a "crisis averted" calming tone, "Oh boy, Genevieve. You don't just have a nasty gash. You're on your way to some dang ugly bruising."

"I bet I'll turn 12 shades of purple," I responded. "Look at my IV hand. It's all different colors."

"I'll put butterfly bandages on that cut across your cheek." Jane stared down her nose at me and continued, "I don't think you'll need stitches, but I'll call Dr. Borlasa or whomever her attending is and get someone to take a look." Jane pressed the call button. "Your CBC showed some serious platelet deficiencies yesterday. Have you ever had a transfusion?"

I told her I had, a long time ago. A CBC is short for Complete Blood Count. That's what the yick and a stick is for every day. They like to keep a close eye on which cells are dying. The bad cancer cells are supposed to die. But they don't go without a fight, they take an awful lot of the good, keep Genevieve alive, cells along with them. You kill too many healthy cells before the cancer's all gone and you need a transfusion. Sometimes you still die, like that first chemo patient, JD. But not so much as back then. They know an awful lot more now.

Still, check out the bone marrow donation statistics. I'm sure it's no surprise, I can't stop myself from reading up on the subject. More times than I like, the cure kills the patient along with the cancer. I knew a tween – that's what they call kids that aren't kids anymore but aren't teenagers yet – she was up on the eighth floor with me. She had gotten a bone marrow transplant in Cincinnati.

When she was in her bed next to me, she had her whole family gathered around her. Several of them would cry off and on. A couple of hours after her arrival they put the tween on a ventilator.

Then her doctor came into the room. She didn't have Dr. Borlasa. She had a male doctor I'd never seen before on the floor. I don't know, maybe I had seen him. But he'd never worked on my cancer.

Anyway, he told them that there was nothing they could do for her. All the tests showed that she was cancer free, but the radiation they had given her to kill all her bone marrow before the transplant had damaged her lungs. She had come home from Cincinnati a few weeks earlier and caught an infection. Tragic.

He told them, "There's nothing we can do."

Worst words of all – ever – in the world. "There's nothing we can do."

Everybody started crying then. Then a woman who looked like three of the other women in the room, only older... I think she was the grandma. She said, "Hush and stop crying. Say your good-byes to her. I know she can hear you. Tell her you'll miss her, and you'll see her down the road. Tell her that Paw-Paw is waiting to greet her when she's ready to go."

Or she said something like that. I just remember that it worked. All the other grown-ups were rubbing the tween girl's arms and hair and telling her they loved her and to have fun with PawPaw.

When I woke up the next day the little girl and her family were gone. I don't know the rest of that story. Well, I think I probably do. But nobody ever came in and told me what happened to her. Doesn't matter. I figured it out.

Sad.

Wait. I didn't finish telling you about my bloody mess.

Yes, change subject. That memory makes me sad. And a little bit scared.

So, anyway, Nurse Jane said I'd probably need a platelet or plasma transfusion. Or maybe whole blood. But she didn't think so. And then a man and a woman came in the room. I guess they must have responded to Jane's pushing on the call button. Jane asked the woman – another nurse, I think – to get a hold of whoever was on call and see if he or she could come look at my face.

Then she introduced me to the man. He was an older guy in a two-piece grey uniform. They looked like scrubs, but I'd never seen the nurses or docs wear grey before. "Genevieve, this is Wallace. Wallace's from housekeeping. He'll help me clean up this little mess you made."

I looked over at his kind face. "I'm sorry Wallace," I said.

He smiled the biggest smile and told me not to fret. That's the word he used "fret." Wallace thrust his hand at me, "Pleased to meet you." Wallace spoke with a large warm voice – the kind you'd expect Santa to have – except he looked way too skinny to be Santa. "I've met you before but you're always asleep when I do," he explained. Wallace told me he comes in every night and straightens up my room.

"Oh, so you're the one who keeps this place so spic and span!" mom had come back to the real world and was doing her best to act normal. She thanked Wallace for helping her daughter. "You aren't willing to come home and keep her bedroom straightened up for us, are you?"

She was talking too loud and fast again, but Wallace didn't seem to mind.

He looked back at mom, smiled, cocked his head to one side and shrugged his shoulders like he was considering it. Then he busied himself around the room while the nurses shined lights in my eyes and checked my reflexes.

After about 10 minutes, my face had stopped bleeding, and Wallace had collected all the bloody linens and wiped down the floor and bedside.

"Why don't you sit in that chair by your momma, Miss Genevieve," Wallace asked. "I'll get the bed made up and you can catch a few more winks before the sun comes up."

Jane told us that there wouldn't be any stitches. My face should heal "just fine." Then Jane told us the even better news, "What's more important: your port seems to be working well, so we'll be getting rid of the IV later today... and the nasty pole that tripped you."

When Wallace was all done, he helped me back over to the

bed. Then he bent down to one side and picked you up and put you in my lap. I hadn't even noticed that in all the confusion you and about three other schoolbooks had flown off the bed and onto the floor underneath. Blood splatters covered the top one.

"Uh oh," Wallace said, "Now you have a bloody history book." He frowned a little and continued, "I guess that's kind of appropriate though. Don't you think, Miss Genevieve? After all, history's such a bloody subject."

He wiped the blood off the book the best he could. He put it – and the other uncontaminated volumes – back in my hands proclaiming, "There! Safe and sound!" Then he left the room.

Wallace called back over his shoulder, "I'll see you again Miss. Genevieve. But with any luck you won't see me. This is a heck of a way to have you be awake during third shift. And I sure hope we don't have a repeat."

The nurse gave me something to relax me. She also said I'll have a sore face in the morning and the relaxing medicine would help with the pain too. I know one thing. I'm getting drowsy. They sure have good sleeping medicine in this place. I hope she gave some of it to Mom.

G ood Day, Miss Flynn,

Allow me to introduce myself. I am the Tsarevitch, Alexei Nikolaevich. My father was Nicholas II, Emperor of Russia. More importantly to our discussion here, my mother was Empress Alexandra Feodorovna, granddaughter to the British Queen, Victoria.

My great grandmother, the queen, had a genetic disorder now known as hemophilia. At the time she was born, scientists knew nothing of this disease or how it spread. Hemophilia is a sex-linked recessive genetic disorder. That means that people may inherit the disease if their mom has it and the baby is a boy. Or if both mom and dad contribute an X chromosome that carries the disease; then a girl may be born with the disorder. As I'm sure you already know, a person requires two X chromosomes to be genetic females and an X and a Y to be genetic males.

Most people inherit hemophilia, but not always.

In a rare stroke of bad luck, one of my great grandmother's X chromosomes mutated. A rare disease, hemophilia spontaneously occurs, like Victoria's did, in 30 percent of all cases. That means that while only one in five thousand persons have hemophilia, one in about 16,000 people get the disease from a sudden genetic mutation. Before my great grandmother was born, there were no known cases of hemophilia in her family. And prior to my mother marrying my father, and having children, there were no known cases in the Romanov dynasty. I have sisters who carried the gene but because my father did not have the disease, he gave them all a normal X chromosome, so they could not get the disease themselves.

My parents were anxious for a son. After four daughters, their wish came true, and I was born. Their blessing was also a curse. I was the first and last male of my father's line born with this debilitating blood disorder.

Because Great Grandmother Victoria had nine children, and her children went off to marry nobility across the globe, royal families throughout Europe shared the gene. As these children intermarried with other monarchs, the condition spread.

The evolution of medical science has, over time, unlocked many secrets to disease. Genetic diseases, such as mine, remained mysteries until the latter half of the last century.

I thought I would share the details of my illness with you because of your unfortunate bleeding spell today. I'm sure you already know that hemophilia causes uncontrolled bleeding. What the chemotherapy has been doing to your blood stream, genetics did to mine. While our conditions differ – I lacked a clotting factor, and you have depleted cells – the outward effect is essentially the same. Because hemophiliacs have our condition from birth, we have many more negative side effects than your doctors expect you to confront. For example, our bleeding – like yours – can happen under our skin. Subcutaneous bleeds don't just cause bruising for us. Our joints and muscles also fill up with blood. As a result of this increased vulnerability, my father assigned two navy officers to care for me at all times. They protected me the best they could. But little boys fall down. Little boys jump up and down. Little boys overexert themselves. Following these playful episodes, my joints and muscles would fill with blood and leave me with incapacitating pain and immovable limbs.

Often my security detail carried me around our residence when the blood pooling in my joints and muscles prevented me from walking.

My sisters treated me in a kind and loving fashion. I feel awful that you don't have sisters or brothers. I think they would be a comfort to you.

Because I was the only son of Nicholas and Alexandra, the entire family bore an enormous burden to keep me alive. I do not doubt they would have loved me and done the best for me, no matter the situation. But the laws in my country required a man assume the throne and this doubled the intensity of their protective measures. I was the only male heir.

My sisters could not rule as Elizabeth or Victoria of England had done. Generations before me, jealous and egomaniacal men passed a law prohibiting women from running the empire. The men of the 18th century despised another of my female antecedents, Catharina II. It was their sexism and resentment that denied my sisters any opportunity to rule.

You may know Catharina II as Catherine the Great. It is ironic that I had one successful and powerful grandmother with flawed genetics that doomed me as her heir and another efficacious matriarch whose empirical success denied my sisters their ability to claim the throne.

Over the years, political forces around the world have whittled away the number of monarchies, my Romanov family included. Few of the remaining monarchs – the ones in power here in your time – retain any real power. Political forces now demand that governing be done by the ordinary in cooperation with each other. Perhaps that is because – in part – these royal diseases proved that we are all ordinary. I am no more superior a human being than a boy from your country named Ryan White. In fact, Mr. White accomplished far more remarkable things than I, in his short lifetime.

By 1971, when Mr. White was born in Kokomo, Indiana, doctors understood hemophilia. They diagnosed him at three days of age. Medical science had advanced a great deal in the half century since my death in 1918. Scientists learned which clotting factor we lacked. In an effort to overcome this deficiency, doctors treated hemophiliacs, including Mr. White, with blood transfusions.

I know they are talking about transfusing you tomorrow. Do not let this story alarm you. Science has progressed even further since Mr. White's time.

Back in the mid-20th century they found that transfusing a hemophiliac reset their blood streams for a little while. The transfusions also reduced the number of joint and muscle bleeds. Young people did not have to endure the pain and difficulty I had when moving. Not so much anyway.

Early transfusions used the entire blood product collected from other humans. As scientists learned more about whole blood, they distilled out the clotting factors, concentrating just the coagulating part they needed. This innovation made transfusions quicker and easier on the patient.

Ryan White received weekly transfusions.

Then tragedy struck. His clinicians transfused him with blood infected by the Human Immunodeficiency Virus. Yes, the same HIV that killed another of your visitors, Arthur Ashe, killed Mr. White. In fact, because the Red Cross blood supplies went untested for HIV for so long – (I know what you are thinking. Clara Barton would be horrified) – half of all hemophiliacs in Mr. White's time became HIV positive.

That is a staggering statistic – brought about by the distillation of coagulants – and ignorant politicians. Instead of getting blood from one person, a hemophiliac could get the collected and combined contributions of 20,000 donors. If one of those donors had HIV, the entire sample would be contaminated.

Mr. White caught the virus. Like Mr. Ashe, it didn't kill him right away. Mr. White lived for five and a half years after a bout with pneumonia revealed his HIV diagnosis. He did not waste any of his limited time. Mr. White went back to school. But the non-scientific community often allows their fears to control them. When school officials learned of Mr. White's illness, they tried to expel him from his studies. His parents filed a lawsuit and they won. By the time of the court's decision the brave young man had captured the attention of the world. He was hated and loved for his unwillingness to go into hiding with his disease.

His passing touched many. One ordinary Indiana schoolboy had more influence and impact on his generation then my royal existence ever did. Famous individuals from all around the world attended his funeral.

Miss Flynn, you have such amazing technology at your fingertips. You can see on computers the many artists, musicians and politicians who attended his funeral. And, in what seems like magic to those of us from the early 20th century, you can watch interviews of Mr. White speaking to reporters and giving hope to others. I encourage you to do so.

Miss Flynn, until next we meet.

Or as my countrymen say, до следующего мы не встретимся

Alexei

OH! WAIT! One last thing. Do not be afraid of the woman who came to see you with the cards. My mother, in her fervent desire to keep me alive so I might one day rule Russia (and no doubt, because she loved me) sought the assistance of a village faith healer named Rasputin.

Many people have assigned sinister intentions to this man. I know nothing of Rasputin's politics. I only know that he encouraged my mother to stop listening to my doctors. You have learned how useless medicine was more than a hundred years ago. It was worse than useless in my case.

These doctors, out of ignorance, had given me aspirin for my pain. Miss Flynn, I am sure you know, doctors give old men aspirin now to protect them from heart attacks because it thins the blood.

Rasputin saved my life.

Did he know why or how? Perhaps not. Granted, he did not save it for long. But this piece of advice – to stop complying with the doctors – was immeasurably helpful to my condition. Just because someone's purpose is not understood, it does not make them less valuable. You may not understand the woman with the cards. But I think she has a message yet to share.

I opened my eyes in my still dark room to see someone sitting in the chair across from me. So much has happened in the last four days, I didn't know what time it was, what day it was, and I sure as heck couldn't tell who that person was sitting against the wall.

What a messed-up way to wake up. The infernal heat was back, and my sweat had soaked through my t-shirt. I didn't know what the temperature might have been, and I wanted to find out. But no dice. There was no way I was getting out of bed to check the thermostat with that person over there. Even though I didn't need covers, I pulled the sheet up from my legs to cover my torso.

"How can you stand this heat?" the person asked.

It spoke. I recognized the voice. But, in that "Gee I just woke up. Who the heck is in here with me?" state, I couldn't pinpoint her identity.

I should have rung for the nurse. But, from the heat, I knew I had a new Magic Diary entry. I couldn't be sure this person was even real. Could someone have just written me a letter and then **decided to hang** out with me before leaving? If she turned out to be a visitor from beyond, calling the nurse would ruin any chance I had of finding anything out about her. **After all**, when I first woke up, I didn't know my most recent visitor had been a 14-year-old monarch in waiting, and not a grown woman. I hadn't even read the post yet.

It sure would have been a trippy turn of events if I had come face to face with one of my magic diary visitors.

But, on the chance she was terrestrial: a real live person who came to mess with me – as real as you or me (Well, not you MD, you're a diary. Albeit real but not of the person variety) – I still couldn't ring the nurse. She could have been the person writing the messages and cranking the heat. I might still get to the bottom of why she would have taken up writing in some poor kid's journal and pretended to be all those other people.

So instead of ringing for help, I said, "Why don't you turn the light on, and we can see what the thermostat says? You could even turn it down for me, if you don't mind."

She got out of her chair and that's when I saw that she wore a baseball cap. "Mrs. Mattingly?" I whispered.

Then the light flicked on. Sure enough, Mrs. Mattingly. No Martha Washington. No Abigail Adams. No Tokyo Rose. Just the nice old lady with the tarot cards.

"What on earth are you doing here? And what time is it? How long have you been sitting here? Where is everyone else?"

Mrs. Mattingly answered me in reverse order, "I don't know where everyone else is. I've been here about 20 minutes. It's getting close to 1 p.m. and from the looks of things, you haven't touched your lunch. Oh, and I'm here because I had a strange experience today and I'm worried about you."

Me? What did she have to worry about me for? I got worrying about me all covered. Thanks anyway.

I'm mean seriously, Mrs. Mattingly. I don't need you even a little worried about me because I'm a little worried about me!

Look lady, I have a lot to deal with right now. To say the least.

In the normal kid category: I'm crazy about a boy who thinks he likes me, but he hasn't seen me with the rest of my hair gone yet. I should just stay away from him before I get any scarier looking because I could be setting myself up for a real let down.

And on the not so normal kid spectrum: I hope to go home in three days (If she says it's 1 p.m. then it must be 1 p.m. Thursday) and that leads me to the astronomically big issue I'm facing right now. Mrs. Welch, the teacher who thought a journal would be a good idea, is coming to see me tomorrow. She wants to see the progress I've made in said journal.

I rolled my eyes.

Mrs. Mattingly responded as though I had said all of that out loud. She smiled at me. "It's my," she paused, I think for effect and then emphasized the next word – feeeling – like that... "It's my feeeling that you should stop worrying and just show Mrs. Welch your diary."

"Are you crazy, I blurted," immediately sorry for my rudeness. But I pressed on, "She'll read all that mumbo jumbo and call the school shrink on me."

Then Mrs. Mattingly earned her keep, as Nana likes to say. Mrs. Mattingly said, "None of us know what's going on – although I have my suspicions – but one of the things we have not yet ruled out is that you (and she pointed her skinny index finger right at me) are writing these visitor entries."

GENIUS.

That outlandish old lady cut right through all the other details – like the fact that the fires of hell breathe forth every time an entry is made. (Although I suppose I could be doing that too, sleep walking or something and turning up the heat). Besides, I don't have to tell her about the heat. Mrs. Welch doesn't have to know anything except that my Magic Diary is filling up with interesting information and it's keeping my mind occupied like she said it would.

Mrs. Mattingly continued, "All the entries follow along with the experiences you're having. It's plausible for you to have surfed the internet until you found these interesting people to study. Then you spiced up the things you learned by pretending that these interesting subjects of your web searches are writing to you."

"And she already knows I want to write fantasy stories when I grow up," I shouted.

Mrs. Mattingly chuckled and whispered, "Shhh, you'll get me thrown out of here for getting you all worked up."

I lowered my voice but otherwise continued as if she hadn't spoken. "Although my fantasies were about little kids with acne and little cartoon characters that cheer them up. Voodoo dolls that giggle when someone tickles a child. Nothing like this."

"Well, no one in their right mind will be surprised that your attitudes about things have matured," she kept talking in a voice that said I should've figured some of this out for myself. "Let's face it. You've had to reconsider some very serious issues. The last time you thought about them you were so young, you couldn't grasp what they all meant."

Now she looked like she felt bad.

I'm a bit of a mind reader too at times. I could tell that she almost couldn't believe that she'd just reminded me about my cancer and its cruddy prognosis. Relapse recoveries are a lot rarer than curing a cancer the first and only time you have it.

Mrs. Mattingly looked down at her hands and in that instant her face got 15 years older and a whole lot sadder. Yeah, this time she seemed to know what I had been thinking, "That's why I'm here, Genevieve. I've had some very difficult visions since I saw you last."

Man. Even though I don't believe she can tell anything with those cards of hers. I've got to tell you, her attitude got so scary so fast. I couldn't help but get a little afraid of what was on her mind, even though I knew she couldn't see the future.

Mrs. Mattingly had opened a window and the room had turned into an icebox.

I shivered.

She got up and closed the window saying, "Yeah, I agree. It feels a lot colder in here now."

I asked her to tell me the reason for her visit. I kind of felt like she shouldn't have come to see me without Mom or Nana here. She sensed that too.

"I'm sorry if I'm scaring you, Genevieve, I don't mean to. Let me get to the point." I watched her move back over to her chair and sit down. Her posture had corrected itself. She looked quite stiff and her demeanor waxed business professional.

"This morning, I had to do a reading for a woman. An immigrant from the old Soviet Union, she's been trying to learn about her extended family because after the Bolshevik revolution, so many of the records were lost. This woman knows little about her ancestry but remembers visiting her grandparents as a little girl and seeing a few pocket-sized items that her grandmother held quite dear in their otherwise Spartan home. One of them was a gold Star of David. She thinks they might have been Jewish, but she has no way of knowing for sure what religion the family may have been before the USSR was founded."

I shifted in my bed. I must have looked uncomfortable.

"Oh, my goodness, I'm sorry. I'm not getting to the point, am I?" Mrs. Mattingly stated the obvious in a rather apologetic way. "I had her cut the cards, like I did for you, and I started the reading. All of a sudden, I felt this incredible hot flash come over me. "Now, Genevieve, my hot flashes days are over. So, I knew something unexpected was afoot. And then, as I was about to turn over the next card, an image of you flashed into my head."

"Me?" I asked. "Why me?"

"I don't know," she continued, "But you were hurt. I didn't know it, I saw it! Blood covered your entire face and drenched your hair."

Poor Mrs. Mattingly shook in her seat as she spoke. Her eyes welled up with tears. "Genevieve, I didn't know what to do. I wanted to stop the reading. I wanted to tell my client that her reading had somehow been contaminated by another presence, another influence. But I didn't. I perceived some higher force at play. I had to finish her reading."

I felt my hand reach up and touch the big scrape with four butterfly bandages across them. I wouldn't have called attention to them, but her details were uncanny.

Then something occurred to me. She could have been in contact with Nana.

Man, thinking she'd sneaked behind my back and talked to Nana: That's when I realized how cynical I'd become.

Mrs. Mattingly answered my thoughts – again. "I know you don't trust me. I also know that it isn't personal, it isn't about me. All those messages in the diary would blow my mind right about now, too. But I noticed that cut on your cheek when I turned the light on and I must admit, it gave me great comfort to see that my vision didn't result in more damage."

I thought she was done talking when she looked straight into my eyes and added, "No, I haven't talked to your grandmother."

I flushed with a twinge of guilt. I tried to reassure her, "Mrs. Mattingly, I don't think you necessarily want to mess with my mind. But you're right, the idea of a few literal ghost writers is rather impossible to believe." I sighed, "I guess I'm just looking for someone to blame for all those letters."

Mattingly smiled, "*Ghost writers*. Pretty cute, Genevieve."

Once I explained my concerns, once I told her the truth, I felt bad for all my suspicions. I could see she – like Mom – was a lot more worried about my condition than I'd ever been.

I asked her to finish her story.

She had lost her place in her head a little bit so she asked if she could go get a glass of water. I told her that would be fine. And it would give me a chance to look in here and see who had come by and cranked the heat in my little world.

Mrs. Mattingly did not come back for a long time. That surprised me. I hadn't expected her to be gone so long. When she did come back, her swollen eyes and puffy face implied that she'd shed more water than she'd taken in.

She was gone such a long time, I'd read the message from Alexei and written most this entry before she returned. Even though it fit what she'd been going through – talking to a Russian and all – I didn't tell her who had been here making my most recent entry. But I did ask if she'd mind if I wrote while she spoke. I told her I'd begun quoting people in my journal and this way my quotations could be more accurate.

She asked if I'd mind just taking notes on what she said and writing the entry later. That way if, for any reason, I didn't want to write everything in here, I could weed stuff out after the fact. I thought that was a decent idea and told her it'd work just fine.

When I agreed she reached into her bag and pulled out an identical notebook to the one Mrs. Welch gave me. She said, "Here, this can be for your notes. I brought it in case you wanted to fool Mrs. Welch with a fake one. But I think our idea to use the real one and blame all the writing on you, is much better."

I marveled at the new notebook. I couldn't believe my eyes. Had my magic diary looked like this just last week? Wow. So much had changed. Well, the Magic Diary had just gone through chemo with me, I suppose it deserved to get ragged looking too.

I've also noted a change in me that's profound like the change in the diary. Maybe I can't deny Mrs. Mattingly's observation: I'm maturing.

For example, I've noticed that I don't feel like I'm writing to this book anymore. Writing to "it" – like it's alive. "Hey, MD," and all that. No. It feels wrong. I'm **shifting** to the third person when I refer to my journal. Perhaps Mrs. Welch will be proud of me for remembering the literary points of view.

I guess as long as I don't go all omniscient, I'll be OK. The folks who write in here are remarkably all-seeing though. I've noticed when they give me advice. They know about stuff that happened after they died. And they know about me. Weird.

So yeah, I guess if I'm the one writing all these entries then I've already written in the omniscient point of view too. Hey Mrs. Welch, if you read this far, do I get bonus points?

Nonetheless, (I looked that up in a thesaurus. Nonetheless is a synonym for anyway. And I write anyway way too much) … Nonetheless, I looked over at Mrs. Mattingly as she sipped the tea she'd brought back from the cafeteria. I thanked her for the new notebook and asked her to finish her story.

Mrs. Mattingly started in the middle of the thought she'd left an hour before, "I looked over at Alyona. That's her name Alyona Vladimirovna. Oh, maybe I shouldn't have told you that."

I shook my head like it didn't matter. Because it didn't. Mrs. Mattingly continued, "I couldn't tell if she knew that I had been so jarred by my vision: by seeing you all bloody like that. But of course, she did. And of course, she thought the beads of sweat on my forehead and my alarm were all about her. I assured her that our reading had just been interrupted by my concern for a new young friend. But somehow it still didn't feel like I was telling her the truth."

Mrs. Mattingly looked worried again. "Truth be told Genevieve, it felt like that reading was about both of you."

"Alyona asked me to continue. So, I turned over the next card. It shocked me to see the Knight of Pinnacles. Now that wouldn't have been an earth-shattering card for a young man, or someone with boy children. But why Alyona? Or why you, even, Genevieve?"

My mind went straight to Roger. An instant later, I scolded myself. *Ridiculous, Genevieve. Mrs. Mattingly did not break out in a hot sweat over your love life.*

"Tell me about him," I said. "Tell me about the Knight."

"Well," she explained. "He's not earth-shattering. He's not original. He's kind of motionless. He has a great burden. He's the kind of person you wouldn't even think of if you hadn't met him face to face."

"Or if he hadn't written in my diary?"

Mrs. Mattingly concentrated for a few minutes. "Well, I suppose. Why? Who wrote in your diary?"

I got a little snarky and I asked, "Don't you know? Why don't you tell me?"

Mrs. Mattingly waved her hand at me and gave me a good-natured smile. Then she said, "So I turned over another card. That one was the four of swords. I can't tell you how relieved I was to see that card. The four of swords means you can stop worrying for a while. A truce has been called. There will be no more danger to face until you are ready to face it."

"What if I'm never ready to face it. Am I out of danger?" I asked. Now a little eager to have her mumbo jumbo cards be real.

Her eyes softened. "I don't know, Genevieve. I bet on most days you can handle anything. All I know is that when I saw that card, I knew you were no longer in immediate danger."

"Then I turned over a third card: The Wheel of Fortune. This card signifies change." Mrs. Mattingly looked overwrought. "I have to tell you, this card mystified me. More change. What change? How much more change could we all endure? Did the card mean I should change my focus back to Alyona? How could that be? Since I sensed that this all had something to do with Alyona as well.

"So, I asked Alyona. 'What have you been able to learn about your name?' I had asked her to look her name up on genealogy sites. 'What did you learn?' I had hoped she had found something that would help me explain what I had been feeling."

This part intrigued me. I urged Mrs. Mattingly to tell me what Alyona had learned. "Nothing useful, I don't think. She said her last name, Vladimirovna, can be traced to modern day Spain now. It's believed to be the name of some nobility that fled old Russia. They are thought to be descendants of escaped members of the Romanov family.

"'But that's crazy," continued Mrs. Mattingly. "I know a little about world history, and the Bolsheviks killed the Romanovs in 1918."

I stared at her. I couldn't speak.

Mrs. Mattingly cautioned me, "Don't look them up Genevieve. It's a very sad story. The soldiers killed the whole family. Even the young prince and his four sisters. The boy had died a gruesome and tormented death. His mom and dad always made him wear jeweled undergarments because he had some crazy thing wrong with him and he was susceptible to injury. These undergarments protected him from the bullets, at first. And he watched his whole family die. When the soldiers realized he had survived the firing squad, they shot him in the head."

Oh Mrs. Mattingly. You don't want me to look it up, so I won't be depressed? Then you tell me the story anyway? Yup, you are a piece of work.

I didn't scold her though. She'd been through enough.

Instead, I riddled her with questions, "Do you think Alyona might be a member of this Romanov family? Royalty from Russia? Do you think one of the dead people who writes to me might have known you'd be seeing her? Is that what you think might be the connection here? Doesn't she have any family you could ask?"

"No." Mrs. Mattingly replied. "She's all that's left of her family. She had a brother, but he died of AIDS in 1991."

I stared at her. Alexei, did you know when you wrote in my diary that the lady with the cards would be talking to your relative. Can't be. The Romanovs weren't Jews.

"Mrs. Mattingly, would you do me a favor?" I asked. "Sure, if I can," she replied.

"It might be uncomfortable, but I need you to do it. Can you ask her how her brother contracted AIDS? And then come back to see me."

The nurse just left. I'm scheduled for a platelet transfusion at 8 p.m., this evening. She said the good news is that afterwards, I shouldn't bleed as easily or be so sleepy.

I don't know that I want to stop sleeping half the day, anymore. That's when my most interesting friends come to visit. I used to fear sleeping. I used to fear my cancer would win. I used to fear that the day would come when I'd fall asleep and never wake up.

Boy I don't worry about any of that now.

Well, I would if I thought about it long. But I don't think about anything like that most of the time. I don't have time to worry about it.

What about this Romanov relative that Mrs. Mattingly read for? That's who I want to think about. What if her brother got his AIDS from an HIV tainted blood transfusion for hemophilia? That was my first thought. Like Ryan White!

But hemophilia wasn't on the Romanov family side. It was on Queen Victoria's side. What was her dynasty? I'm curious now. I'll look her up on my new iPad. Nana bought me one and had Alma drop it off. She walked in here just after Mrs. Mattingly left. I don't know if they saw each other in passing, but if they did, I'm sure I'll have "a lot of 'splaining to do" when Nana gets back. Nana always says that. It's from an old TV show. "Lucy, you got a lot of 'splaining to do."

BRB

House of Hanover. The Internet is incredible.

Even more interesting though, I put in the name, Vladimirovna and I got a story about "Her Imperial Highness Grand Duchess Maria Vladimirovna," you guessed it, of Spain. Turns out that a few years ago, the Russians invited this woman to come back to her ancestors' country and be a figure of state. They want her to restore some of the "soul" of Russia. They want their spirituality back.

In fact, they want the Romanov Dynasty back so badly that they've offered the duchess an abandoned palace. According to what I read from a translated story in *Izvestia*, she can take her pick of two abandoned castles. One of them is in St.

Petersburg and the other is in – wait for it – CRIMEA! I wonder if it's near Nightingale's hospital.

Whoa, man, this diary just gets more trippy every day. I feel like having a party and inviting all these dead folks to hang out together. Nightingale, meet Alexei. Alexei, meet Nightingale. Time has woven your lives together right up to 2015 when Alexei's 12th cousin was invited to live in Crimea. Nightingale cleaned up a lot of the mess made by that war. How's this for irony, Alexi? It's a war that your Russian great grandparents fought with Great Britain. You know, the same Great Britain where your great grandmother was queen. Besides all that, how's that the hemophilia she gave you?

Oh right, the hemophilia. Alyona, I thought your brother might have hemophilia if you were a Romanov. But he wouldn't have had hemophilia. Hemophilia was on the Hanover side. You're all related on the Romanov side.

Unless, like Victoria, he or his parent or grandparents were one of the 30 percent of hemophiliacs that result from spontaneous genetic mutation. In that case it would be just an amazing coincidence.

It wouldn't surprise me though. I've gotten to the point where I'm almost expecting amazing coincidences.

Like Mrs. Mattingly doing the reading of a Tsarist relative and successor the same day that Alexei Romanov visited my diary.

No, that wouldn't be coincidence, that's spiritual messaging.

Coincidence is my subconscious writing that message from Alexei the same day as Mrs. Mattingly's reading for Alyona. Yeah. That's a coincidence.

But Alexei said in his letter that there are no more Romanovs. Could he have been wrong about that? Not so omniscient after all then. Yes, just a coincidence.

Is there any coincidence without spirituality? Are we all interconnected anyway? Even if it isn't physical? Even across the centuries? Do we operate in relation to the existence of each other?

I heard once that Albert Einstein didn't believe in

coincidence. He said, "Coincidence is God's way of remaining anonymous." I'm sure he said it, because I looked it up. But I find it hard to believe that Einstein believed in God.

I don't believe in God. Maybe that's why I find it hard to believe that Einstein did.

Nana and mom are stopping at FATBOY'S to bring me dinner tonight. They have amazing milkshakes and these killer Canadian bacon BLTs. Too bad my appetite's shot. I guess that's why they are stopping there. They're trying to bring me something irresistible.

I'll try to eat.

Then I'll get my transfusion.

Then tomorrow, Mrs. Welch comes. I'm nervous about that. More nervous than anything else, right now. Considering I have acute lymphoblastic leukemia, that's saying something.

Nana says Mrs. Welch promised to be here early. Before school. So, she won't miss her first period homeroom. I used to be in that homeroom. Seems like centuries ago.

I don't mind getting up to see her. Aside from my nerves about her seeing my diary, I'm excited she's coming for a visit. She may be a teacher, but she's one of my favorite people.

Now that I have an iPad, I'll set the alarm to wake up at 5:15 a.m., that way I can get a shower before she gets here. One more shampooing should finish off the rest of my hair. Nana bought me a new Cleopatra style wig. It's pretty. And I've never had jet black hair before. So, it makes me look a little mysterious, I think.

Here comes mom and Nana. Mmmm, that smells good! Later!

G ood evening, Genevieve,

I suppose it's rather predictable that I would take advantage of your trip down to the 3rd floor for your transfusion. I think it's likewise predictable that I would write to you after you quoted me earlier. As we've already determined, coincidences are how god remains anonymous.

So, no coincidence, I'm next in the line of your many enchanting visitors. And no, I don't think I was sent by God. I don't think you should think so either. I do, however, think we exist in the same universe, you and I and God, but not on the same plane. At least not under ordinary circumstances.

Do you know much about my theories of relativity? I think they can help us understand what's going on here.

I had two theories of relativity and from these I built many other hypotheses. From these I postulated many more truths.

I began with my theory of special relativity and then I perfected my theory of general relativity.

Special relativity is like it sounds: specific. Here's how it works:

Supposing you and I are on an airplane. Let's say the airplane travels at 450 kilometers per hour (km/hr). We are both on the airplane, so you and I are traveling at 450 km/hr, as well. But we look at each other, and it looks to us like we aren't moving at all.

Even if you and I sat on the wing and felt the wind in our hair – proving to our senses how fast we traveled, the minute we looked at each other, we would look – relative to each other – like we were still **quite still**.

So, let's move our imaginary selves back inside the airplane. The light inside the plane is moving around at – well – at the speed of light. The speed of light is a little over a billion km/hr. 1,079,252,848.8 km/hr to be exact. While inside the plane, the light moving front to back would travel 450 km/hr faster, or 1,079,253,298.8 km/hr.

But it can't.

Light can't do that.

Nothing can.

Nothing can move faster than light. So, if you or I tried to travel at a speed additional to the speed light travels on its own, something else would have to slow down. According to me, that's time. Time must slow down.

I think I may know what you are thinking. Why do you care? Trust me, I get that quite a bit.

Am I right? If I am, please indulge me another moment and let me explain. Remember our goal is to put you and I and God (and Florence Nightingale, my old friend Harry Truman, Arthur Ashe and everyone else) back into the same plane of the universe.

See, if I succeed, time slowing down will prove itself a very important part of our discussion.

But before we get to people of another time moving into your plane, let's work on proving time's relativity in a much less ethereal way.

Let me use your new iPad to explain it.

(On a side bar, Genevieve, I must tell you how much I would have loved this iPad. You should have seen the computers in my day! Big as a house and they couldn't do a fraction of the computing that this one small gadget can do).

On your iPad you have a map. In my "time" (and I shall now use that word very subjectively) a map was drawn on a piece of paper to show the topographical and physical reality of an area in question. A human would look at the map and plan a route.

Distances were estimated based on the scale to which the map was drawn. There would be a key in the corner of the chart that told you, for example, that two centimeters equaled one kilometer. Humans would navigate the available routes computing the time necessary with a series of simple equations once the average speed at which they would travel had been determined.

After a certain amount of planning, the journey could begin.

This is nothing like the map you have on your iPad. Your iPad navigation system need only know your destination. It selects a route or gives you options and you select it. And then the computer software gives you a series of commands so you might arrive at a predetermined time. In addition to that, your map – and here's where I come in – knows where you are.

Your iPad is in constant contact with a satellite orbiting the earth. This satellite contains equipment that monitors your speed, location, and obstacles along your route. This satellite uses equipment called a Ground Positioning System or GPS. Might I add, by any standard, all of this seems miraculous.

When I was five years old, I got a compass for a gift and I thought I had discovered the magic of exploration. Imagine if I had seen an iPad!

Now here's the hitch. That satellite is up in space, circling the earth. It's moving incredibly fast. In fact, it's moving about 14,000 km/hr. And no, it's not right above you. In fact, it doesn't stay above any one spot on the planet. If it did, it would be geosynchronous, but it is not. You've got more than one GPS at various spots around the globe bouncing information back and forth between your iPad and their computers, taking each satellite's location into consideration and compensating for where and how you should go.

The GPS satellite doesn't just have computers. It has an atomic clock. An atomic clock is a very precise instrument. It calculates time based on the element cesium's frequency wave. Your iPad on the earth's surface is synced up to another atomic clock here on the ground.

When we add 14,000 km/hr to the maximum speed of light energy, we discover a real imperative for time to slow down. And it does slow down. That's the reason for the two atomic clocks. They sync up so you can be given the correct information on where and how to go, based on the speed of time on the earth's surface versus the speed of time in space.

Up in orbit, the average GPS satellite loses about seven micro-seconds per day. That's a tiny amount, but it's enough to get you lost or take a wrong turn if that satellite can't relay and receive accurate information to and from your iPad. So, my special theory of relativity has a daily impact on everyone's 21st century life. Even if individuals lived without an iPad (and I don't know why they would want to), GPS technology allows for everything from underwater expeditions to pizza delivery. And at one time or another in your century, everyone will use special relativity or suffer without their favorite pepperoni calzone.

You're welcome.

Now for my general theory of relativity. This takes all of that bending and slowing and pulling of time onto a grander scale. Onto a universal scale. This explains the pull of the fabric of the universe to make room for bodies of enormous size and mass. It stretches the plain upon which a celestial body rests. The way a fish in a net pulls the net out of shape.

The face of the matter is, Genevieve, I'm on one plane. You are on another. There is a time where I exist. It's just that in most cases neither you, nor your grandmother, nor your teacher, nor anyone else from your time can meet me because you are on a different plane. You exist on a different layer of the universe bending your own fabric of space.

Although now, it would appear, our layers have overlapped.

You would have thought such a thing impossible. But for centuries scientists thought the things I understood about physics were impossible. Take for example my general theory of relativity, it wasn't until an eclipse blocked the sun in 1919 that anyone could see the way the stars were stretching out of their expected position because of another enormous body in the sky. In that case, our sun.

The genius mathematician, Sir Isaac Newton, would have said the sun's gravity pulled other enormous bodies out of their plane. But we now know that each enormous body stretches its own plane out of shape. Gravity proved not as simple a concept as his 17th century understanding would have us believe. Perhaps one day Newton's and my planes will overlap, and I can explain my discoveries to him.

Enough of this, Genevieve. You don't want a physics lesson. Besides, I don't make a habit of teaching things I don't quite understand myself. And while I do understand general relativity, what I do not yet understand is how one layer could have been bent so far that it intersected with another layer.

That lack of understanding – our layers overlapping – that is where I lay all my references to God.

Because of my willingness to defer to contemporary language about such things, people are constantly speculating that I believed in god. They wonder if I prayed to him. Or her. Or it.

Genevieve, I would never presume to know. I would never speak with certainty about anything I could not prove with mathematics or science. But the people of my "time," believed in an anthropomorphized deity. When I spoke to them of things greater than themselves, when I theorized on things grander than their understanding would allow, I stumbled. I used the language they used for such things. And yes, as a result, many people assigned the mysteries of the universe as I explained them, to this anthropomorphized creature of their own design.

For example, when I was asked how random quantum affects influence quantum mechanics, I responded, "God does not play dice with the universe." Dice is, of course, a game relying on the probability of random occurrences.

It seems too few people got my point.

I chose that language because I thought it would be helpful if I spoke in words that ordinary people used, to help these big concepts make sense. But, instead of clearing up one simple physics question, I opened the door to hordes of speculators surmising about faith, my faith and the existence of one unique creator.

So, Genevieve, I'm not telling you to believe that God put us together. But I want you to know these two things: The universe bends and time slows down. Did I catch up to you? No. I don't think so. More likely, somehow, you slowed down to intersect with me.

Perhaps the friction from all that deceleration is where the warmth in your hospital room originates.

Genny, forgive me. You don't have time to worry about how this perceived time travel happened. Save that for another day. Perhaps you can study physics in college. For now, when marveling at the wonders of the universe, go forward without hesitation. Don't worry about these messages being original. Just study the messages for what they bring to you. What theories can you form from your new knowledge and expanded scope?

I would like to share one final observation with you. It is an emotional reaction to the time in which you live.

I want to share my surprise. In all likelihood, I have no right to be surprised. Not after all these years of having my words twisted by others to validate their version and vision of god. But, surprised I am none the less.

Perhaps dismayed is a better word.

In my lifetime, I would have imagined that, by now, humanity would have learned to be better to each other.

Had I given the 21st century more thought, I would have expected more advancement. Religious wars and religious scapegoats should have been put behind mankind by now. And why have you not put greed behind you? I would have expected a society in which no amount of money justified any level of human suffering. People of the 21st century still starve to death. Still die without necessary medicines. I find this remarkable – humanity's one true indictment.

The World Wars of my lifetime appear to have taught subsequent generations nothing. And for that, I am truly sorry.

What's in your future, Genevieve? Will you have a Genevieve's theory of general relativity? Have you learned from your Magic Diary that the force we exert in the universe changes the way other bodies act around us? Arthur Ashe pushed back against apartheid. Ryan White pushed back against exclusion of sick children from school. But then Jim Thorpe couldn't push back enough against human ugliness and prejudice. The weightier bodies around him pulled him off course.

Sigh.

Oh, I almost forgot! Congratulations on this Magic Diary. I understand how it feels to have something no one else does. Even if it is only your own experience or just your imagination.

In 1905, when I was 26 years of age, I published five groundbreaking papers. One of the papers included my special theory of relativity and the now legendary equation E =

MC^2. I called 1905 my *annus mirabilis*, my miracle year.

Again, with the language of gods or magicians. My miracle year. Your magic diary.

No matter.

My life has always been charmed. As a young man, I wrote to my sister Maja, "If everybody lived a life like mine, there would be no need for novels." Genevieve, I sense you **know** exactly how I felt.

With cordial best wishes,
A. Einstein

T his is Nana.

I'm writing in this until Genevieve wakes up and can write for herself again.

Something went wrong during her blood transfusion. I've seen her get these before. I wanted to watch again because the transformation from tired, run down, poisoned little girl to lively petal spreading flower creates such a sense of hope in me. Watching a person over doped in chemotherapy get new blood looks like those time-lapse videos of a flower blooming.

I'm heartbroken to say, no flower bloomed tonight.

They started the transfusion and within minutes Genevieve's face flushed. Then she started shaking. Genevieve complained that her back hurt and then she went into full blown convulsions. The nurses seemed to know exactly what to do. They disconnected the IV bag and replaced it with saline. They said they needed to flush the vein. It looked like they would just push the offending blood product through her body.

I asked them if they were forcing it into her body that way. The hematologist said they had no other way to get it out of her.

Genevieve – in considerable pain – stayed strong and calm. My poor daughter, however, required sedation before the whole fiasco ended. She's sleeping in the empty bed here beside us.

In the middle of all the controlled chaos, Genevieve seemed to get confused. She thrashed around asking us to turn the "bright lights" off. She vomited twice and then drew her hands up from her sides and clutched her head. Her fever continued to spike and after a few minutes she became unconscious.

Like she is now.

The doctors and nurses seemed perplexed by that turn of events. They've come back here several times since returning Genevieve to her room. They've been honing their theories of what went wrong.

I've been told that there can't be one explanation for everything. They believe that two strokes of bad luck happened at the same time.

I can't wait for her to wake up so I can tease her about being an over achiever, as usual. I'll cajole her with a little, "Oh Genevieve. You need to get better so we can put this creativity of yours to better use."

But for now, we know the underachievers that did the blood typing for her plasma infusion got it wrong. They think she had an acute hemolytic transfusion reaction or AHTR. Genevieve keeps track of all the giant names they give her conditions. Everyone remarks how she has the vocabulary of a 60-year-old woman. I suppose some of that is my fault. But we can also give credit to her daily ingestion of multisyllabic medical jargon.

AHTR happens when the plasma antibodies are incompatible with the recipient's red blood cell antigens. The nurses said pure human error causes this to happen, usually when someone mislabels the blood product.

Most patients don't pass out when this happens. Renal failure is the big concern in cases of AHTR. They called in the nephrologist to check Genevieve's kidney function. See, for a kid with cancer and some already compromised systems, the danger of serious permanent kidney failure is frighteningly high. They told my daughter and me not to worry too much. They gave us a form to read and fill out. The last line read, "Fatality rarely occurs in these cases."

The nurses – in an effort to reassure us - explained, "Only about 20 people a year die from AHTR."

Of course, Genevieve had grabbed her head and passed out long before the nephrologist even got in his car to come to the hospital.

Now, it's true what Genevieve has written about me: I'm a tough old bird. I do well under extreme pressure. So, when they hollered that Genevieve was "stroking" I grabbed my daughter and headed for the hallway. Rachel didn't want to leave her baby. But when the hospitalist who had gotten there during the calm "force saline" moments of the crisis told us to go, she complied.

It all happened in the blink of an eye. They pulled the pillow out from under her head. They put something else in her IV. I forgot to ask what. I'll get that big word for Genevieve another time. Then, I couldn't see her through the glass window in the door anymore. Too many people worked around her bed for me to see anything.

It must've been 10 minutes before the hospitalist came out to talk to us. That's something new, hospitalist. Or the title is anyway. They are doctors who work exclusively in a hospital.

Dr. Hassan came out with one of the nurses. He's the kind soul who prescribed the valium for Rachel. My poor daughter. She literally couldn't hear him talk to us. Her quiet hysteria had taken over her conscious mind. They say personality traits skip a generation. In our family it has to be coping skills.

The nurse by his side came back with a little paper cup and a glass of water. Rachel calmed down quite quickly after that.

Dr. Hassan told the nurse to get her another one for 2 hours from then so she could sleep. I still have that one in case she wakes up agitated.

She'd fallen asleep the minute her head hit the pillow when we came back here. Panic dumps so much adrenaline into your blood stream it's exhausting when it wears off.

As for Genevieve, Dr. Hassan told us he believed Genevieve had a reaction to the transfusion. He said we were lucky her symptoms came on so fast and they did not transfuse her all the way. He's waiting on the kidney specialist to tell us what sort of permanent damage might have occurred.

Then he told us there was more. It appears Genevieve's also had a stroke. Dr. Hassan reminded us that strokes are more common in individuals with clotting problems. Could be a stroke, could be an aneurism. Bottom line: it won't matter what he said until we get the results of the MRI. I guess they'll do both. An MRI and a CAT scan. There are some big words for Genevieve. Computerized axial tomography which, I hear, is just a fancy kind of x-ray.

Oh, they're here to take Genevieve down now. I hope the next entry is made by the little wonder woman herself. I sure do.

G enevieve,

My name is Elizabeth Ann. I'm here to tell you that many people are praying for you right now. I don't know what you think of prayer. For me, prayer filled dark and difficult parts of my life with safety and security. I believe, in the case of those who wish to intercede on your behalf, prayer does the same.

Critics of our supernatural belief in prayer don't understand the power it has.

I will share my story with you. It won't take long, and I hope it gives you two important things to think about.

First of all, you are very loved. I am not here because of one prayer. I am here because of a chorus of voices pleading for mercy and for comfort – for you, your mother and your grandmother.

Remember, prayer need not be asking for things. Many of the messages reaching the heavens are from people who love your courage, your stamina. They praise your entire family for your good cheer and gracefulness.

Secondly, I encourage you to stay open to the change happening around you. Today has become an especially difficult day. Your mom and your grandmom witnessed a major setback in your treatment. They are afraid. If you cannot pray for your own recovery, then at least concentrate on it. Focus on the joy you find in each passing day and accept each one as a gift. You may find this meditation more helpful than you can imagine. A mind and spirit at peace are easier to heal. Let go of the fear that contributes so intensely to your pain.

Now a little about me. Just before the founders signed the Declaration of Independence, my parents welcomed me into the world. Rich Anglicans, they raised me in wealth and in their religion. I married into another high bred Anglican family. (Today you would call us Episcopalians). My husband and I raised our own five children in addition to seven of his brothers and sisters whom we inherited when his father died.

You've already learned that colonial America struggled with

many – then mysterious – contagious diseases. Nearly all of them had been imported from western Europe where most of our ancestors originated. Almost everyone in my family suffered from one of these illnesses.

Tuberculosis made my husband gravely ill. In a vain attempt to allay the symptoms, we moved our family to Italy so he might convalesce.

I know that your family has rejected organized religion. And now that I am no longer living as an 18th century woman, I understand the belief that there is more than one exclusive route to God's love. But in the early 19th century, I found in the Roman Catholicism of Italy many answers and comforts I had never felt as an American Anglican. When my husband died, I continued my studies of Catholicism. In 1805, I converted.

When I returned to the United States, my former peers shunned me. As a widow who needed to work – to feed herself and her family – I became the head mistress of an all-girls school. When people learned of my conversion, they withdrew their daughters from my care. I faced great financial hardship.

Before long, word of my religious work circulated through our community, outside the Anglican Church. New parents brought their children to me. Catholic families put their girls in my school. I founded the first Roman Catholic parochial school in the nation. Realizing the need to care for children who had lost their parents, I opened the first Catholic orphanage as well.

I had truly been blessed. I wanted to dedicate my life to God's work. I founded the Sisters of Charity. We were the first religious order of the young United States on the North American continent.

Believe me Genevieve, I am not a great woman. I spent much of my life struggling with fears and mourning the deaths of those I loved most. Two of my children died as their father had. There were times when I would have liked to hide from the world, but I had work to do.

I loved my husband. I loved my children. I loved my students. I loved my orphans. And I loved my God. It was my constant devotion to Him that allowed me to serve all these smaller causes. Genevieve, I prayed every chance I got.

At just 46 years of age, I too succumbed to tuberculosis.

That was 1821. In the years since my death, my followers have named schools and universities after me. One hundred and fifty-four years after my death, the Holy Roman Church declared me a Saint.

Genevieve, if I am a saint, then everyone who overcomes their fears to love without question or reward and continues in peaceful service to others, is a saint. I know what you are thinking. Yes, that would make your mom a saint.

That would make all three of you saints.

I have no doubt that your grandmother will laugh heartily when she reads that.

Genevieve, I leave you with my Anima Christi. It's a prayer associated with me by my church. I realize it may not give you comfort. But know that devotions such as these helped me and continue to help others. Genevieve, I will do for your family what I did for my own loved ones. I will continue to pray for peace in your hearts.

Soul of Jesus, Sanctify me.
Blood of Jesus, Wash me,
Passion of Jesus, Comfort me.
Wounds of Jesus, Hide me.
Heart of Jesus, Receive me.
Spirit of Jesus, Enliven me.
Goodness of Jesus, Pardon me.
Beauty of Jesus, Draw me.
Humility of Jesus, Humble me.
Peace of Jesus, Pacify me.
Love of Jesus, Inflame me.
Kingdom of Jesus, Come to me.
Grace of Jesus, Replenish me.
Mercy of Jesus, Pity me.
Sanctity of Jesus, Sanctify me.
Purity of Jesus, Purify me.
Cross of Jesus, Support me.

Nails of Jesus, Hold me.
Mouth of Jesus, Bless me in life, in death, in time and eternity.
Mouth of Jesus, Defend me in the hour of death.
Mouth of Jesus, Call me to come to Thee.
Mouth of Jesus, Receive me with Thy saints in glory evermore.

Elizabeth Ann Seton

N*ana, please show this to your daughter, Rachel. I have written it for her. Thank you.*

Mrs. Flynn, I am sorry to see how sick your little girl is. I hope she is up, reading this and writing journal entries again, real soon.

It's my hope that I can convince your daughter and your mom to let you read her "Magic Diary." It would be good for you. You'll be proud of her. Like you always are. You will understand how she's able to enjoy her time in the hospital. I know that perplexes you, just now.

Nana, I know you are already tempted to show this diary to your daughter. You think it will have the same effect on her that it's had on Genevieve. It will keep Mrs. Flynn's mind busy and give her something to fixate on besides all these scary medical issues that face your little family.

Here is another reason you should show Mrs. Flynn. When her teacher, Mrs. Welch, reads it, she will have lots of questions. Of whom will she ask those questions? Why, Mrs. Flynn, of course! Then the cat's out of the bag either way. Am I right?

Yes. You know I am.

Now, Mrs. Flynn, now that you're reading my message, I need you to do something. I am begging you to do something. And you need to do it for Genevieve.

Please believe me. What I'm asking you to do is the most important thing possible right now.

Remember, I am begging.

Please please, please come to terms with Genevieve's mortality. I guess that sounds like an odd request coming from a dead little boy.

You must understand. I watched my father grieve – inconsolably – for 48 years. When he died on the 28th day of March in 1969, his last thoughts were of me. He did not pass from this world thinking about my mom or my siblings.

He had long before said goodbye to his own beloved mom.

His winking conscious thought did not reach out to his brother who protected him when they were just children. Even though, that young man had saved his life back in their teen years.

He did not pass away reminiscing about his tenure as the Commander of the Supreme Allied Expeditionary Force or his responsibilities as Supreme Allied Commander of the entire European campaign.

His two terms as president, filled as they were with success, did not consume him. No, his thoughts went to me.

You see, Mrs. Flynn, my father never dealt with my death. Consequently, it haunted him far worse than you might accuse me of haunting you, right now.

Mrs. Flynn, I am Doud Eisenhower, the first-born child of Dwight and Mamie Eisenhower.

My parents hired a young woman to work around our house. Remember what Florence Nightingale told you about nurses in her time. Many young impoverished girls cleaned the houses of the more comfortable in society. While my parents would never have been considered wealthy in their early years, it was customary for mothers of a certain social status to have in-home help with their household duties and their children.

My parents hired a very poor young girl to move in with us and care for our house. And, here is why my father obsessed about my death so – they never checked her background.

I am very proud my parents weren't afraid of robbery or shiftless behavior. I am grateful I had parents that trusted the poor. Many others feared that the lower financial classes consisted of amoral or dishonest types who would pilfer purses or pinch the silver.

But in the 1920's our society knew so little about science and medicine they misunderstood the threat around them. They should have feared a different villain. They should have feared disease. My parents never dreamed death could come at the hands of the 16-year-old girl they hired and brought into our home: because she brought with her, scarlet fever.

Within a few days of exposure to this innocent young girl, I fell ill. Not long after that, I died.

My parents grieved my passing. My father, inconsolably.

A career military man, my father had been all over the globe. My mom could live anywhere. She chose Colorado. We lived there at the time of my death. They buried my little boy remains there.

Decades later, after what critics have labeled, *the finest public service career of the 20th century*, my father sent for me. Regardless of his role as father, husband, statesman and military hero, he could still hear me crying to him from a small grave at Fairmont Cemetery, in far off Denver, Colorado.

In 1966, he had my body exhumed and moved to the small chapel at the Eisenhower Presidential Center. He stood there, with his hat in his hand, and watched them lower my remains into a new grave. One near him while he lived. One sharing the space where he would be buried, just three years later.

The year after my exhumation and reinternment, my dad remarked that my death had been "the greatest disappointment and disaster" of his life. Confiding that it was, "the one I have never been able to forget completely."

This is the point I think your daughter tried to make to my dad's old rival, Harry Truman. Everyone dies – well – everyone dies one at a time.

My dad, the supreme allied commander of that war with 30,000 deaths – daily – knew that each of those persons had the same value as his little Doud. And if he had had the capacity to feel about them all, the way he felt about me: his heart, like yours, would have shattered into 51 million pieces. His heart would have shed another shard for every Doud who died in that war.

Mind you, Mrs. Flynn, at the end of his life, he did not punish himself for what critics describe as his blunders. He could not concentrate on World War II or Korea or his legacy in French Indochina – what you all call Vietnam. He chose not to think about how many had died on his watch. No, instead he focused on the one little person who died because he was not watching. I died because he didn't check on our poor little maid and make sure she was healthy enough to work.

Mrs. Flynn, I believe my passing destroyed what little happiness he might have had in this world. When I died, it darkened every good day he spent as a cattle rancher on the edge of the Gettysburg Battlefields. It darkened VE day. It darkened his presidential inaugurations.

Mrs. Flynn, I love my father. Let me assure you, that affection I feel means I know how much Genevieve loves you. Because of that intense love, I have come here to beg you to stop mourning her mortality.

I will not pretend to know how you can do it. If the most powerful leader of the 20th century could not accept his child's death, I do not know how to expect you to do it. I just know that it will be the most wonderful gift you could give Genevieve.

You must overcome this crippling sorrow. Do not pretend to accept that her cancer may shorten her life. If you fake it. She will know. It is possible my father had more courage than any other living man. He faced down his enemies, and they relented. But I, the one person who never felt anything but love for him, I defeated him.

I know you want to comfort me. You want to tell me scarlet fever defeated him. How foolish to allow a disease to define your life. Do not let Genevieve's illness defeat you. Do not let it define you. Look at Genevieve: it does not define her.

Trust me when I tell you this: I would rather not have lived.

I know Genevieve's condition has worsened. I pray she recovers long enough to see the change in you. I dream your daughter will wake to find you by her bedside, strong and encouraged by her zest for life. Genevieve's wisdom and love have already defeated her cancer. Whether her body survives it or not.

I pray that you will have the chance to show her that you too, will triumph, no matter how severe the loss.

With great affection,

Doud

This morning, about 2:00, they moved Genevieve to intensive care.

Wallace, the housekeeping associate who had lovingly kept her room clean, moved her personal belongings up there himself. He gently placed her clothes, shoes, schoolbooks and this precious diary in the closet. Genevieve's MRI and CAT scans showed a small brain bleed. Her doctors hope she will recover and have no lasting cognitive impairment.

Genevieve's Nana asked why they thought she'd be, "Just as smart as ever." The neurologist explained that the bleed appeared to be confined to the cerebral cortex. That part of the mind controls physical movement. Her ability to move and regulate those movements might not work as they always had. But physical therapy could help.

Her Nana's one remark: "Good. Because we all love Joe. He'll get her back up to speed."

I didn't come here to see Genevieve. I had no intention of leaving her a note. I'm drawn to room ICU-34. I came to see a 31-year-old male with a gunshot wound to the chest. His Aunt Rebecca called out to me. She's immersed herself in her memories of me so she might find comfort or clarity from what happened to her nephew.

When I get those calls from people suffering, I set down beside them. I try to make my presence felt. I try to cross the barriers that separate us. I hope to comfort them.

If you could draw a picture of me in their room, I'd seem like that little bat Genevieve pictures over her mother's head. The one she has been picturing since she first got cancer. I'm sure someone like me fluttered there many times before and insightful little Genevieve picked up on him or her. Seven-year-old Genevieve even tried to attach an identity and draw the character.

I haven't gotten to room ICU-34 yet. I don't know what horrible circumstances reminded that 31-year-old gunshot victim's family member of me. Although, it appears senseless violence had something to do with it.

On my way, I passed by this room and felt as though I had a second calling: one that came from this closet.

I've never seen a child appeal to so many of us. I'm impressed by the souls that wrote to this one sick kid. She must be quite a girl.

At first, I didn't know what I could add, Genevieve. Now I know. I too just want to talk to your Momma.

I agree with Doud, Mrs. Flynn. Stop fearing loss! The weight of your sadness pulls on Genevieve's universe. It bends the fabric of her layer of time. It slows down and contributes to the agonizing parts of her journey. In part, this is what Albert Einstein was trying to say. Don't be a weighty body in her universe, pulling her fabric out of shape with the enormous gravity of your fear.

Escaping into this diary has sped Genevieve's life back up to a normal healthy pace. It does what Mrs. Welch said it would. Writing in her diary helps Genevieve make time pass more quickly.

Your sadness slows her down. It compounds her suffering.

I'm not heartless. I don't say this to hurt you. I have a very different experience from Doud's. I know a different way from the one of inconsolable suffering.

Don't get me wrong, my family grieved my passing too. Total strangers still do. But Momma aired her grief in public for all the world to see. My family didn't carry me like a wounded secret treasure in their hearts the way President Eisenhower did. They talked to others about me. They opened my casket. Momma wanted the world to see what my killers had done. She revealed to the world the broken swollen face of her boy. Momma wanted everyone to know that savages had murdered her son. She did it so that fewer parents would know her grief.

Momma kept me alive in a way that President Eisenhower never dreamt of doing. Momma used my death as fuel in an ever-growing civil rights movement. She turned her grief outward and pushed it into the world that killed her son. Eisenhower never spoke of his son's killer. He didn't go on a public health care campaign. He didn't work to stop infectious diseases. Instead, he buried his sorrow. Instead, he dedicated himself to stopping Hitler. No doubt a free world is grateful to him for his sacrifice.

Although if you ask Nightingale, either way he'd have saved lives.

Still, that sacrifice of keeping silent meant that President Eisenhower never dealt with Doud. His avoidance cost him dearly. President Eisenhower never took a healthy look at his own life's accomplishments. He spent too much time regretting the actions he believed cost his son his life. President Eisenhower thought he'd been derelict in his duties as a father. Something a great general would never have allowed himself to be.

The President wasn't unique because he blamed himself. Momma blamed herself too. She blamed herself for letting me go visit my Grandpap in Mississippi. She blamed herself for thinking a 12-year-old northern boy could handle the phenomenally backward deep south. She blamed herself for not demanding that my Grandpap keep me by his side at all times. Momma blamed herself for forgetting the detestable racism she'd grown up with as a child.

But she blamed my killers more.

Perhaps my death would have defeated Momma if I had caught some awful bug and died. If I hadn't been pulled from bed by two angry white men who thought I'd catcalled the bigger man's wife.

If I'd had something as arbitrary as bloodstream full of cancer instead of an innocent face and a carefree attitude that infuriated my killers, then maybe Momma would never have found her voice. In her voice she found her forgiveness - forgiveness she granted to herself.

Like cancer or scarlet fever, my killers never felt remorse for taking my life.

Perhaps if they'd just been a disease, Momma would have accepted her loss and faded into the background. Perhaps she could have accepted my murderers. These guys, these brothers, they were no more concerned with me than a cancer is mindful of its victim. Anyway, and either way, the end would have been the same. I'm still dead. But because Momma found her voice, she knew that my death wasn't the end. She committed herself to making my death the middle of something bigger than my life.

See, when I was about your age, colored men in the deep south couldn't talk to white women. My cousins took me to the general store near the cotton fields where they worked. The shop owner's wife was tending to the store. I said a few things to her. My cousins laughed. They pulled at me and we ran off. That night, the married 30-year-old white woman told her husband I had grabbed her. She said I spoke vulgarities to her. She told her husband I had catcalled her on the street - in front of my cousins - for the whole world to see.

I didn't mean any disrespect by talking to that white lady. I had no idea that southern whites got so angry at colored boys for things like that. I was born in Chicago and things didn't get so out of hand. Besides, the world was changing. We didn't respect bullies. Or so I thought. Just a few months before I was born Japanese bullies picked a fight with the biggest toughest country on the planet. You and I both know how that turned out.

I should have known better. Genevieve, back in 1941, the U.S. (though poised to become the world's greatest hero) harbored plenty of homegrown villains. A whole lot of the rough and tumble swagger the United States laid claim to sprouted from her intense racism. Headlines called the enemies in the Pacific, "Japs" and "Nips." The government locked Japanese Americans in concentration camps.

By the time I turned 14, the U.S. had finished fighting enemies abroad and many bullies doubled down their racist attacks back home. So, back in 1955, when this northern born black boy said something to a white married lady, her sharecropper husband and his brother decided to teach him a thing or two.

Apologies to your Nana, not the nice way she teaches a thing or two.

The men went to my Grandpap's house looking for me. Grandpap, an obedient old colored man came into the bedroom and roused me from my sleep. The brothers threw me in the back of their pickup truck and drove off.

I took a beating the likes of which no one should ever even try to imagine. They searched the back of their truck and found a fan blade from an old cotton gin. That blade weighed half what I did but they made me carry it to the side of the Tallahatchie River. There they punched me and kicked me until I lost an eye. They made me take off my clothes. Then they shot me in the head and wrapped a rope around that gin fan and around me. They rolled my bloody broken bruised body into the river. A few days later someone found it.

Folks urged Momma not to make a fuss. She wouldn't listen. Instead she had a public funeral with an open casket. She wanted people to see what those barbarians had done to her boy.

For three plus years the FBI kept a case open about my death. The coroner wrote an 800-page report. But none of that mattered. After a jury found my killers *not guilty,* the murderers sold their story to *Look* magazine. That's where Momma learned the truth about how those men tortured her boy.

Even though it infuriated her when she learned they'd gotten $4000 for telling the details of how they tormented and executed her son for talking to a white woman, Momma was glad to know the truth. Their confessions ignited a call for justice. Putting my swollen face out in a public funeral was a revolutionary act and Momma wanted her boy's murder to spark a revolution. Momma did a good thing.

Genevieve, I'm feeling guilty that I've dallied here, writing in your diary so long. I've got to leave for a moment and visit room ICU-34. If they're all right, I'll come back.

I'm back. I went down the hall and turned the corner for room ICU-34, just in time to watch Trayvon Martin walk in. Wow. The family must be inconsolable.

I moved closer to the room and I saw the victim. Forgive me my surprise, Genevieve, but it startled me. He was a white man. Maybe it shouldn't have, but it flabbergasted me. I don't see the sense in it.

You know who Trayvon is?

Trayvon Martin was a colored high schooler made famous when he was shot at close range by a self-proclaimed neighborhood watchman. The watchman drove through Trayvon's neighborhood and observed him walking down the sidewalk. A colored boy in a hooded sweatshirt looked suspicious to the watchman in his fancy neighborhood. When the watchman called the police for help confronting the colored boy who walked just ahead of his car, the watchman was told to stay put - in his car - and wait for the officers the dispatcher would be sending.

How I wish that watchman had listened.

Within minutes Trayvon was dead, powder burns on his jacket, with a bullet piercing his left lung and shattering his heart.

Like my killers, Trayvon's killer went free. All of them found *not guilty*; all of them returned to their homes unharmed. Although Trayvon's killer has trouble staying out of jail. Trayvon's killer keeps getting arrested for beating people. See, unlike cancer taking just one child, Trayvon's killer could kill again.

No one ever blames the child with cancer for getting sick. But Trayvon's killer's defense required that his jury believe Trayvon deserved to die. The defense said Trayvon attacked the watchman. They acted like Trayvon had somehow asked to be killed. My killers felt I had asked to be killed too. Racists seem like small people, but they always have their eye on the bigger picture. My killers believed the colored men who picked their cotton would rise up and demand better treatment if word got around that a twelve-year-old colored boy had cat-called a white woman.

You see the difference Genevieve, don't you? No one would ever have been cruel enough to tell the Eisenhowers that their kid got what he deserved because they didn't screen the nanny well.

Who knows if Momma could have gotten over my death if she hadn't had to defend my honor. Momma took on the herculean task of showing the world that her boy was victimized to preserve a racist status quo. Trayvon too! The acquittal of

Trayvon's killer preserved the notion that colored boys were disposable when their lives get put up against the actions of white men.

Trayvon's parents, like Momma, spoke out against the senseless murder of their son. They highlighted the injustices wrought upon their family. They spoke about their son's murder to anyone who would listen. They went to the media. They even wrote a book.

Genevieve, I believe that the sale of the gun that killed Trayvon might have wounded his family as much as the murder itself. When Trayvon's murderer profited on his death it fueled outrage like the fury that surrounded my death. Some nameless person purchased the gun that killed Trayvon. He or she paid $139,800 so he or she could own the weapon used to exterminate a young colored man. The men who killed me got $4000 from *Look* magazine for the story of how they did it. If a gun's as good as a confession, then Trayvon's killer got paid too. But $4000 in 1956 is only worth about $36,000 now. So, the bounty on colored boys appears to have gone up.

Perhaps the $103,000-dollar difference is because Trayvon's murderer's expensive trophy has changed hands and is somewhere, loaded, ready to kill again.

Maybe that's why he got called here tonight. Maybe Trayvon's killer sold his Kel-Tec PF-9 9mm to another psychopath and now it's shot that 31-year-old gunshot victim in ICU-34.

Would that be why someone would buy a gun with such intense unearthliness? It might be. It wouldn't be the first-time guns had karma. Many folks use their uncle's rifle to go hunting, "Because he always got his deer" with it. A weapon that always makes its mark is a good find for a killer.

So yeah, I stepped back a little when I noticed all the white people around this white man's bed. I watched as Trayvon stood there comforting one young white man. Leaning in the doorway, my eyes met Trayvon's. He nodded and so did I.

Then the white man, the one that Trayvon hovered beside said, "We'd only been married nine months when the guys moved in downstairs from us in our apartment building. You know, they'd pestered us when they had a few drinks or whatever. Then, about three weeks ago, our dog started having seizures. The vet asked if we had lead paint in the house."

A woman sitting near the man speaking rubbed his shoulders. I think Trayvon wanted her to, because he wanted to. Her nephew needed comfort.

The speaker continued, this time he couldn't control his tears, "Then William Randolf Hearst died. He just died. A three-year-old Jack Russell Terrier doesn't just die of lead poisoning in brand new apartment complex."

"I begged Steve not to go down there. I begged him to just help me find a new place. I didn't care if we broke our lease. He said it took too long to find the place we had and that those 'bastards' wouldn't get away with it."

"They shot him. Oh God Rebecca, they shot him." He rocked his head forward onto his husband's bed and wept the way Dwight had for Doud.

Love is love.

So, I came back here: to finish writing. We have a long way to go, Genevieve.

But let there be no mistake. Trayvon's crime, like mine, like the guy in that bed, was having the nerve to act as though being different didn't make a difference. I take nothing away from Jackie Robinson. But when he crossed the color barrier, millions of people watched. Even though he was publicly persecuted for his courage, having all those witnesses saved his life.

Trayvon walked in a gated community with a pocket full of skittles, and I told an attractive white lady she was pretty. No witnesses. No lives saved.

You and your Momma and your Nana are so full of courage. I know you'll pull out of this brain bleed thing. And so, what if you are a little motor impaired. As long as there's no bullet in your heart or your head, you got this.

I know, right? Who thought you could make a joke about a bullet?

But Genevieve, we can. Because you got this.

Take good care of yourself and your Nana and your Momma,

Emmett Till

Genevieve woke up today.

I read her all the posts she had missed. I think being unconscious has made her emotional. She balled her eyes out when she heard what Doud had to say. Then she cried again, for Emmett and Trayvon. She's tired but she's OK.

Her left side is weak. Her fingers and toes don't respond the way they should. Dr. Borlasa said her reflexes on that side were down to a four. I don't know what that means, but "down to" implies not up where they should be. Still, nobody seems upset. They're all just a lot happier that she's awake again.

Oh, and Genevieve agreed to let her mom read her diary. Rachel will be here in about a half hour. I had sent her out to get us milk shakes when Genevieve woke up, so I could read Genevieve the new entries.

In the end, Emmett convinced her. Leave it to a 12-year-old boy to get to the heart of things. Once Mrs. Welch reads that diary, there'll be questions to answer, and my daughter will have to answer them. Of course, by the time Rachel's done reading, she may have more questions than answers. Still, I know Rachel will cover for Genevieve, even if she doesn't know why she's doing it.

Plus. Genevieve agrees, this diary is too engaging to keep from her mom.

Genevieve seems a bit overwhelmed. She knows everything that happened to her. And she only had one comment, "At least my right side still works fine. Tomorrow I can write again."

Today is Sunday. Genevieve lost two full days. Mrs. Welch had to postpone her visit. She's coming tomorrow. Things are happening fast now.

My daughter's back with milk shakes and Roger's with her. I'll let Roger and Genevieve visit for a few minutes while I take my daughter down the hall to show her this diary.

Nana

I guess mom stayed up all night reading. When she first got here with the milkshakes, Nana tried to take her to the family room, she resisted. Then Nana said, "C'mon, Roger and Genevieve want to talk." Mom's a sucker for romance. How does a little bald girl fit into her Cinderella way of looking at things? I'll never know. But it worked. She left with Nana so I could hang out with my 15-year-old Cohen Middle School prince charming.

I like Roger. I like him more than I thought possible.

There, now this sounds like a diary!

I know I've only seen him twice outside of school, but he's dreamy. And not just because he's cute. He's kind. If Nana says I sound like an old lady when I talk, Roger acts like an old man when he interacts with others.

When he walked in with mom, I didn't even try to hide my hairlessness. Something about being awake for the first time in two days made vanity seem trivial. After we got past all the discussion about my recent flirtations with deadly complications, Roger asked me about Mrs. Welch coming to visit. I told him I couldn't wait to see her. I told him about my new Cleopatra wig.

He asked me where I kept the thing. I pointed to the closet door. I actually had no idea where Nana put the wig. But it was as good a guess as any. Roger found the wig box and brought the wig and a hair brush over to me. He bowed slightly and stiffly, like an Egyptian guard, "May I put this on your sacred melon, my Queen?"

Roger smiled mischievously.

His goofing around felt awkward, but his face had this adorable shine to it, and I said, "Yes. If you want to."

He put the wig on me and then he brushed the hair. He pulled back away from me a little and said, "You look lovely." Lovely? What an old man word. But sweet. He helped me up so I could look in the mirror on the wall. I felt lucky to have such a strong Egyptian guard.

The wig looked pretty. Nana did a good job. So did Roger.

Then a nurse came running in. It seems my bed had a sensor in it that went off at the nurse's station if I got out of bed.

She nicely – but sternly – told me to lay back down.

I don't know what their plans are for me. But I guess, for now, I'll ask permission if I want to move around too much. Anyway – Goodbye ancient Egypt – back to my 21st century hospital.

Roger and I talked about school and junk for another hour. Then Alma came to the door. She said Nana had asked her to give Roger a ride home. Roger came over to the bed and kissed me on the cheek. It's a good thing I was laying down. That's all I know!

He looked into my eyes and said, "Farewell, for now, my Queen." Roger made cancer Cleopatra swoon. He's such a sweet adorable guy.

After Roger left, I rang for the nurse to come back. I asked her how long I'd be here. She said if I had an event free night, they'd move me back to the eighth floor in the morning. I asked her if the intensive care unit had many people in it with me.

She replied, "There are two coronary artery patients and a couple of accident victims." She had no idea why I asked. So, she tried to make a little joke of it. "How come, little miss wants to know? You thinking of throwing a party?"

I got scared.

I said, "No gunshot victim?"

The nurse looked startled. She said, "Why do you ask?"

I answered, "Someone had told me there's a gunshot victim on the floor. Room 34, I think."

Then the nurse looked down and said, "I guess it doesn't matter what I tell you. It'll be in the paper in the morning."

I asked her to explain.

She said, "We did have a gunshot victim. He didn't make it. He died shortly before I came on my shift. I came in at noon."

I started crying again. Then the nurse looked like she felt bad. "Did you know him?" she asked.

I answered, "No, but we had some of the same friends."

She offered her condolences and walked back out into the hall.

I lay here wondering why I'm still alive. After a little more than a week of relapse, senseless death seems much more likely than survival. It feels like I'm the luckiest person alive for every extra day I get.

My mom? I don't know what she's thinking. She read the diary. Brought it back. Kissed my forehead. Went to Nana's handbag and took out the extra Valium and downed it with a paper cup full of water from the sink. Then she pulled out the recliner chair, put her hand under my IV hand and fell asleep.

Nana and Alma went home right after that. Everyone is so exhausted but me. I've slept for two days. So, I've got energy I didn't know I had. Besides, I think I'm having a mild anxiety attack. Mrs. Welch will be here in six hours. Heaven only knows what she'll be thinking when she leaves.

D ear Genevieve,

I'm Stephen. I died this morning up the hall from you. I'm
OK. But my husband may never recover. His name is Paul
McCoy. He loves to do things for other people. At first, I
thought you could ask him to help you. But you didn't meet
him in time.

We live at 1539 Indiana Avenue, apartment G. I'm sure he'll
move soon. So, you won't have much time. Can you see if your
Nana would bring Mrs. Mattingly to see him? She can tell him
she got called to him by her cards. Get Mrs. Mattingly to tell
him to let this all go. I should have let it go when they killed
our dog. These guys will go to jail for murdering me, I'm sure
they will. But if by some chance they get away with murder.
It still needs to end. And Paul needs to move on. I don't want
him spending his life broken hearted.

Please. Help him. I have comfort where I am going. He's the
one left behind. Not knowing. Please. Thank you.

And yeah, as for your struggle, you got this.

Stephen Reynolds

It's hot again. But not too hot. Still, I'm sweating. I have no idea where the thermostat is in this room. Seeing as it's an intensive care room, dollars will get you donuts the climate control is at the nurse's station. (I must be feeling better – that's a total Nana-ism).

I'm up early. It's dark outside.

I rang for the nurse. She said she'd check the heat for the room and then come back and help me get a shower. There is no shower in this room. It's not customary for intensive care patients to do such mundane ordinary tasks as take a shower. But the nurse checked with the doctor, and they are moving me back to the eighth floor soon, so they won't keep me bedridden waiting for my new room assignment.

She said she'd bring a wheelchair and take me to the shower room in the nurse's lounge. Everybody's so nice on this floor. The nurse said sad days like yesterday – when the gunshot victim died – make it extra special for them to have a kid like me around. They all think – like Trayvon and Stephen – that I got this.

I feel good either way. I'm OK either way. I read the beginning of my diary again. I almost can't remember being worried like that about my mom. No matter what happens I'm leaving her this diary. That way I'll never be gone from her. I know that now. I hope she knows it too.

Don't get me wrong. I'm not giving up or anything. I still want to live and grow up and write fantasy novels. Maybe even get to go on a real date with Roger some time. But for now. I'm OK.

Here's the nurse with the wheelchair.

Wow, that felt great. Hot water pouring over my back. The nurse let me take a plastic chair into the shower in case my leg was too weak to support me. She was worried about me slipping. I sat in that chair for the first four or five minutes and felt the water on my skin. Then I washed my head and felt my smooth scalp. My left hand couldn't hold the soap **too well**. The nurse told me physical therapy would help a lot. Joe will fix me right up.

When the chemo's over, my hair will come back. Last time I lost all my hair, it was curly but grew back in straight. Maybe this time the straight will go away and I'll get curly hair again. Who knows? Hair is hair.

After I put on the clean sweatpants and t-shirt that the nurse got for me out of the closet, I went back to my room in the ICU. I walked in and found Wallace making my bed with fresh sheets. "Hey Wallace," I said. "What you doing changing the sheets? I'm moving back to the eighth floor today." He said he already knew that, but it's still no fun to put a clean body inside a rumpled bed. "And besides, it only takes a minute," he told me.

I asked him if he'd be going home soon – seeing as he works overnights. He told me, "Six a.m. is my usual quitting time. But I volunteered to work late." He said, "I thought I'd help you move later today when the room upstairs gets freed up." He smiled and explained, "I moved your things to intensive care. I want to be the guy who moves you back to the eighth floor." Then after a short pause he added, "I've taken a shining to you, Miss Genevieve."

After thanking him, I wheeled myself back out of his way. He busied himself with the trash can and medical waste containers. Then the nurse shifted me out of the wheelchair and into the freshly made bed. I leaned back and looked up as Mrs. Welch walked in.

She looked great. In school she wore her hair tied-back, but today that mane of hers flowed around her shoulders. She had on a hot pink t-shirt that read, "Never trust an atom. They make up everything." And what a smile on that woman's face! I imagine I had a corresponding happy look on mine.

"Genevieve!" she shouted and threw her arms around me. I hugged her back. She pulled away from me a little bit and said, "You've mastered the art of scaring the heck out of all of us. What was the idea with that little brain bleed business? I hope you're done with all these shenanigans of yours." I promised her I wouldn't be doing anymore frivolous bleeding, if I could help it.

She pulled her backpack off her back and unzipped one of the compartments. "Here, I have something for you," she said.

I did a massive eyeroll in her direction and she said, "Don't worry, it's not more homework. It's a t-shirt. I got it when I got my new one. Do you like mine?"

"Heck yeah, I love your t-shirt," I exclaimed. And I did. It made me smile. Plus, I told her not to worry. I'd never trusted atoms since Mrs. Jennings in 3rd grade told me about them. I had just gone into remission the first time and after school I asked Dr. Borlasa if there were atoms in my cancer. The Doc was so excited by my question, she showed me the atomic structure of my cancer cells.

I looked back at Mrs. Welch's t-shirt and proclaimed, "Atoms can definitely be assholes." Mrs. Welch looked stunned by my cussing and then she cracked up laughing.

She replied, "Truer words never spoke, my young friend."

Then she pulled my t-shirt from her backpack. It had a big sorcerer's hat on it, and it read, "Magic's science that we don't understand yet." Mrs. Welch told me that one of her favorite authors said the quote. His name was Arthur C. Clarke. I told her that my dad liked him too. We watched his movie 2001 about 50 times when he'd stay home with me back in the day.

Her smile faded a little when I mentioned my dad. "Have you heard from him since you got sick?" she asked. I told her I hadn't, but I didn't care. She nodded her head.

It got quiet for a minute.

Then, standing with his back to us, Wallace piped up, "Well, I'm no doctor but I don't think you'd be leaving intensive care if they thought you were going to have another stroke anytime soon. You'll be good as new in no time."

Silence again.

Poor Wallace. That was a nice attempt at changing the sub-ject that worked out to be super awkward!

Then he turned around.

I looked over at him after his lame attempt to lighten the mood. I smiled at him. But Mrs. Welch didn't. Mrs. Welch stood stark still. She stared at him: glared at him – more like it. He walked over to her with his hand out and said, "Hello, I'm Wallace. I'm sorry, I didn't mean to interrupt."

Mrs. Welch stared at his hand. She didn't shake it. Her glance moved from his arm to his face again. "What are you doing here?" she said in a low tone. Her voice alarmed me. She spoke in a menacing way, almost. I can't put my finger on it. But she sounded threatening.

I don't know if he startled her by speaking or upset her by talking about me having a stroke. Or if she knew him some-how. None of this strangeness seemed to effect Wallace one single bit.

"I came to change Genevieve's bed," he said without miss-ing a beat. "I work on the eighth floor, but I've kept her things tidy since she got here last week. So, I'm just following up on my work." Then Wallace turned away from her and smiled at me – as if my homeroom teacher hadn't just gone all freak-out on him and said, "I'll see you later this morning for the move. I'll leave you to your visit for now."

Wallace left. Mrs. Welch just stood there for what seemed like a long time. After I heard the elevator close at the end of the hallway, I broke the silence and changed the subject. I'd seen my parents get angry at each other too many times to pry into what was bothering a couple of grown-ups. Frankly speaking, they get uptight about the stupidest things. And if Mrs. Welch had a bone to pick with Wallace, I'd rather not know.

Bone to pick or missed a beat. Oh my god, I'm turning into my grandmother right before my very own eyes.

So, I said, "Well, I do so like my new t-shirt. Thank you. I bet you'll be glad you got it for me when you read my magic diary."

That snapped her out of it a little bit. Mrs. Welch

brightened up and reached out for the notebook in my hands: the one I'd been taking notes in since she got here.

"No, not this one," I pulled it close. "This is just a notebook my Nana's friend, Mrs. Mattingly, got me to keep track of what people say. Later I copy their comments into my diary. When no one is around." Then I reached under my covers and pulled out the real magic diary. Looking about a hundred years old, the dog-eared pages and constant handling had made the notebook she had given me unrecognizable.

The last defensive look fell away from her face as she reached out to take the diary from my hands, "Wow, Genevieve. You have been writing up a storm."

In for a penny in for a pound, as Nana would say. So, I shrugged off her comment and replied, "Oh, Mrs. Welch, wait 'til you see the storms blowing around inside this book."

She flipped through the pages. "I'll tell you what," she quipped. "I hadn't dreamed you'd make such effective use of the diary..." Her words trailed off as she looked at random entries. "I knew you had a story to tell. All of us do. But a young woman who has lived through all you've experienced... Well, I knew you'd have a lot to write about." Then she looked up at me and said, "All the different handwriting. That's so cool. And it couldn't have been easy to keep coming up with new styles. I love the doodles. I guess handwriting is just another form of artwork to you."

Was she asking me a question? Was I supposed to say, "Yeah, Mrs. Welch, I practice writing with different penmanship all the time. Where have you been?"

I didn't say anything.

She kept pawing through the diary like she was holding a sculpture. Running her hands over the pages. Feeling the ink drenched grooves that the words made in the paper. Then she held the book to her face and sniffed so hard she nearly sucked it into her lungs. I started thinking Mrs. Welch had a few screws loosening up in there.

I still had the Mrs. Mattingly notebook. I wanted to record what Mrs. Welch said about the diary when she realized that so many of those entries weren't mine.

Then she read my mind. "Oh, you're going to write down my responses. I guess I better choose my words carefully then, shouldn't I."

I nodded at her and smiled.

Her face lit up when she saw me smile. "Genevieve, I'm enchanted. I guess that's the point of magic, isn't it? To cast a spell on someone. Well, taking my idea and turning it into hundreds of pages of written word is charming! Bewitching! Find a magical term and apply it."

Her response puzzled me. I asked, "But you have read none of it. How do you know if it deserves any praise at all?"

Mrs. Welch looked at her wristwatch and said, "Dang it, Genevieve. I will be late for homeroom. I can't stay here and read it. But I'll come back. I can't come tonight; I have a chess club fund-raiser to chaperone. Tomorrow night, I'll come back and read it cover to cover. And I promise, if it's no good I'll take back every glowing term I've used today. But I don't think I'll be taking anything back. Have a fun day, Genevieve!"

In a flash, she was gone.

I'm in an intensive care bed and her exiting comment was "Have a fun day!" Mrs. Welch has a bit of the BattyPatty in her, I think.

But the magic diary did its job again. Just by coming out from under the covers, the diary made Mrs. Welch forget whatever her beef was about with Wallace.

Now that might have been the strangest part of her visit. Mrs. Welch taking weird exception to Wallace. I wonder, does she know him? Or perhaps she dislikes people eavesdropping on her conversations. Well, I don't think that was Wallace's fault. He couldn't vanish when she walked in the room.

Yeah, her reaction shocked me. But maybe something shocked her. Something threw her off guard, which doesn't happen too often in her well-ordered world. No matter what it was, it wasn't pleasant. I'd like to avoid that sort of thing from now on. No more knocking Mrs. Welch off guard – at least not until tomorrow night – when she when she comes back to read the diary.

Nana walked in with Joe. Wallace came in right behind them. I had fallen asleep. I looked over and asked what time it was. Joe said, "Time for you to have a little physical therapy. I hear we have a lazy hand and foot in this room. Time to whip them into shape."

Nana said, "It's 8:30 and you're headed to room 812."

Wallace followed up with, "Why don't you take her down to physical therapy, Joe. By the time you get back, I'll have her things moved up to the eighth floor."

I clutched both notebooks with my good right arm.

Wallace added, "Do you want me to deliver them to your new room? Or do you want your grandmother to take them?"

I looked at everyone for a few moments and then I found my words.

"Joe," I asked, "Can my Nana take me down to the physical therapy room in a few minutes. I'd like to talk to her for a quick minute first."

Wallace said, "I know my cue when I hear it. I'll leave the room until I see your grandmother take you out in the wheelchair, then I'll come get your stuff."

I added to Wallace, "I need my Nana to run an errand for me. So, I'll trust you with the books, OK?"

Wallace bowed low to scrape the floor with an imaginary hat. "I'm honored you trust me, your highness. All will be as Your Ladyship wishes upon your return."

Everyone laughed and he and Joe left the room together, "Come on little lord Fauntleroy!" Joe put his arm around Wallace, "Let's grab a coffee in the nurse's lounge here. They always have donuts in the lounge on this floor."

Nana looked at me and asked, "What's up Your Ladyship?" I gave her the don't-get-started eye roll.

I showed her Stephen's post. I asked her to bring Mrs. Mattingly in to see me. She wanted to know why I wanted to see her, instead of just passing on the message from Stephen. I told her I had a few questions. I didn't mention the weird thing about Mrs. Welch and Wallace. But it was on my mind and I thought Mrs. Mattingly might have some insight.

Nana asked how long physical therapy lasted. I told her it would be at least an hour before I got back to my room on the eighth floor. But she could ask Joe. She said she would when she dropped me off. So, I put these two notebooks in the closet and trusted Wallace to take good care of them.

Hey Kid,

I'm here to tell ya that things ain't the way they appear to be. I may be a bit of a heavy hitter to deliver that message. But, hey, I don't get called on to visit the living all that much.

You gotta know by now that all the folks you run into (by the time they're 30 years old) got something they're hiding. Nobody's one hundred percent true. Unless they're some Johnny Low-life. Them guys, you know the minute you start talking to them, you just can't trust 'em as far as you could throw 'em. And that goes double for you. 'Cause a kid like you can't throw nobody, nowhere.

Some guys, and I know some of 'em, they's horrible people. Maybe they was born horrible? But probably not. They just ended up horrible, even by the time they was your age. And there ain't one good thing left about 'em.

But most folks is just kinda bad. They got bad traits or bad things happen to them and they's basically good people, so they hide it. Stuff ain't what it appears. And if you don't run into the problem they faced, you never know the lies they's carrying around in there.

Think about those people that ran the gas chambers in Germany for that Nazi bastard, Hitler. (Sorry kid, my words get colorful from time to time). Those folks went home at night and what did they do? Did they gas the neighbor's cat? No. Course not. They kissed their wife or husband and they patted their own kid on the head. Maybe even tucked 'em in with a bedtime story. Then the next day they went right back to them ovens.

Disgusting to think about, ain't it? But they was just people, right?

Now kid, I hope you never run into anyone with a bad side that bad, but I don't want you to get fooled either. Stuff that don't seem right, probably ain't right. And there's always a bigger story. Sometimes you learn the truth about people you know and sometimes you never do.

Your teacher and the janitor guy, right? Nice people, but

that Welch lady's response when she saw him. It's bugging you. Don't let it bug you. They're both over 30. They got secrets that's all.

I told you I was a bit outta the league around here. I don't want you to think them people you like are guys like me. Well, they are, but to a tiny degree. They ain't got secrets like my secrets.

See, if you'da met me (probably with that tough broad grandmother of yours) you'da thought I was just some two-bit dance hall thug. I peddled booze and broads. Over the course of my career owning gin houses, I got arrested maybe 10 times. Always for some stupid little rule I broke. I let the girls dance after hours or I sold booze after hours. I'd get a fine (about $3) and then I'd get kicked to the curb to go back to my dance hall and make more dough.

Some folks who saw me coming and going with brown grocery sacks full of money, they thought I ran with some bigger dogs. They thought I was the luckiest SOB money launderer in the south, 'cause I never got caught.

I never got caught because I didn't run money for the mob. I ran it for the CIA. And they tended to protect their guys, well, until they didn't no more. If you used up your usefulness, you was gone from their protection.

But I'm getting ahead of myself.

In the early 1960's I delivered money to agents and informants between New Orleans and West Texas. I wasn't no agent myself. I was just an employee. Call me a patriot who ran money for the Central Intelligence Agency whenever they needed it done and they needed it to look like it was just some mob dealings. I got paid. I made about $200 a month as an employee. My bar got hassled seldom enough and I kept money running to the guys who had their eye on them Castro sympathizers or some other guys who watched for other kinds of anti-government activities.

Who was happier than me? Right. Nobody!

Now you're a smart kid. You mighta thought the FBI watched the domestic scene for the government. But the Federal Bureau of Investigation in them days was run by this lunatic named J. Edgar Hoover. And I guess my bosses at the CIA didn't think he and his boys had their eye on the right guys. Hoover got hisself mixed up in the black movements and then the anti-war movements. He pulled up rocks looking for bad guys and got bogged down in their sex lives and social change agendas.

My bosses at the CIA were a lot more interested in starting the wars then in worrying about dirty college kids protesting 'em. And they sure as hell **wasn't gonna** waste none of their time following Hoover around. And the FBI, **for the most part,** returned the favor. I don't think them g-men walked into my gin house three times in 15 years. Unless it was to put a saw-buck in some lady's stocking, if you get my drift.

So, I'm running my business and running cash for the nation's secret police when I get a call to do a big job. Something outside my paygrade. My bosses were looking for a nobody, some lowlife that nobody would suspect… to kill somebody.

Don't get me wrong, kid. I kicked up a fuss. I told these guys I ain't never killed nobody and I ain't got no ambitions to spend the rest of my crappy little life in prison. They told me I'd never do no time. They told me America would love me for it and I could kill this guy on live television and walk away after a few questions.

Well, they got half of it right. I could walk up to this guy (and I did) and shoot him on live television. And when the cops announced to the folks outside, "Jack Ruby shot Lee Harvey Oswald," the crowd went nuts. They was cheering and whooping it up. But Johnny Law came down on me swift and furious. I didn't walk away. I went to trial. Got found guilty. On March 14, 1964, the lying bastards sentenced me to death.

Look kid. I kept my mouth shut. Jack Ruby ain't no snitch. And I shoulda known they **wasn't gonna** care what happened to me once I killed their patsy. And besides. No one wanted to believe anything I had to say.

For cryin' out loud, the **very** afternoon John Kennedy bought the farm, that sniveling know-nothing, J. Edgar Hoover proclaimed the case closed. They had their man. They had arrested Lee Harvey Oswald for the murder of the president and some poor dumb cop that caught four bullets from two different guns. Hoover didn't care about evidence. He didn't care about the truth. His concern for who **really** killed Kennedy (a guy that Hoover hated) was the exact opposite of my bosses' concerns. The CIA cared a great deal about who the killers were: because the agency themselves had done the killing.

So, they picked me to be the stooge to cover it all up.

A few bright bulbs didn't buy the official story that had come out of Washington. One such guy, Jim Garrison, he knew a lot more than my bosses wanted him to know. Garrison, the New Orleans District Attorney, knew lots and lots of stuff.

Never ones to leave too many loose ends, the CIA did a good job of getting to all the notes and transcripts and setting them on fire. Garrison even said on an NBC news special that the murder of President Kennedy got plagued by a rash of "spontaneous combustion" because all the evidence kept catching fire.

He knew about the bullets in Officer Tippet's body being from two different guns. He interviewed countless witnesses from Dealey Plaza. And he scoured the Warren Commission's report. That Warren Commission, now that was a laugh.

Garrison pointed out that the main objective (in the writing) of the Warren Commission was to calm the fears of the American people that their president's murder was a organized crime. They didn't want nobody thinking it was some sort of government conspiracy.

But the CIA and the FBI did a great job making Garrison look like a nutcase. They had people like me telling every reporter who would listen that I loved the president and it was my inconsolable low life grief that brought me to the police department to murder Oswald.

Nobody. Listen **to me, kid!** Nobody who knew me woulda believed that story. I was a gin house thug who didn't care two figs about politics. And murderer? Hell no. I'd never been no gun for hire. My pals knew that I ran bags of money around for hire. And never nothing more.

Look, kid. You don't have to take my word for it. *Playboy* magazine carried a series of interviews with Garrison where he maps out the whole messy plot. And except for a few things he just couldn't know, he got it right. Now I bet your ma and grandma don't want you reading *Playboy*. But see if someone can get those interviews for ya. And Garrison did a few TV interviews. You might be able to see those. But like I said, the whole media machine set out to make Garrison sound like a crack pot. That's why his interview wasn't in the *New York Times*: it was in *Playboy*. All to keep him from being heard.

But in the end, kid, the truth comes out. Oliver Stone made a movie he called JFK and he made Garrison the hero of the show. Well, because he was.

And even before that movie came out, the U.S. Congress convened the Select Committee on Assassinations. That select committee determined that the Warren Commission had rushed to judgment. They declared that there was more than one shooter. They didn't exonerate that poor bastard Oswald, but they should have.

But like I said kid, nobody's gonna tell you the whole truth. Even when they say there's more to the story, they ain't going to unwrite the official word on who the bad guys were.

The good parts of the Committee's report? They tore up the book on the FBI handling of the case. And not just for JFK, for Martin Luther King, Jr. too. They even attached some of the blame for King's death to the FBI dogging him the way they did. They felt that the FBI had set up a culture for killing folks like King. Well, of course they did.

Why'd my bosses kill Kennedy? I think they was pissed at him for cancelling their invasion of Cuba after they botched the Bay of Pigs so bad. Then there was the Commies. Kennedy wanted peace with the Soviet Union. He didn't seem to like the idea of fighting the commies after that Cuban Missile Crisis proved diplomacy could solve the problem.

Kennedy wanted to bring the troops home from Vietnam. I think Eisenhower only sent them there to appease that frog, Charles DeGaulle. Ike thought he needed him to join NATO. DeGaulle needed stuff too, though. His conflict in what he called French Indochina was a big post World War II head-ache. That frog's war broke the French banks. Ike helped him out in Indochina and the frog played nice in Europe.

But like I said, I ain't a big one for politics. Old Lyndon Johnson though. He gave the CIA the war they were after. I wonder how many times they had to show him that Zapruder film before Johnson fell into line.

Ha ha.

I'm sick, I know. But this is how the world works, kid.

As for me? Well, an appeals court decided I didn't get a fair trial. They promised me a new one, outside Dallas, in 1967. Everything was looking like my buddies in the CIA was – at long last – watching out for me. Then some medical guys came to see me. They said they had to give me an injection for a cold. That's not what they did. The CIA had some jokers who did science experiments giving cancer to mice. They worked with a doctor in New Orleans. Or at least they did until some-one found Dr. Sherman hacked to death in her apartment. Somebody went crazy on the broad with one of her kitchen knives.

Now, that's a nasty way to go.

Within a month of my injection for the cold, I was dead. They said it was lung cancer, but I had tumors **all through** my body. My brain, my lungs, my liver.

The CIA don't leave stuff to chance. Me getting a new trial. That woulda been leavin' a lot to chance.

Especially with that Garrison guy nosing around.

Well, little lady. I gotta go. But you keep your nose clean and don't worry about the junk these grown-ups is keeping from ya. You'll have stuff to hide soon enough. And you won't want nobody poking around in your business neither.

Take care, kid.

Your buddy, Jack.
Jack Ruby

Joe wheeled me into my new room. There sat Mrs. Mattingly across the table from Nana. I'd forgotten that I'd sent Nana on a quest to find the psychic, that's how hard Joe worked me. I got out of the wheelchair and grabbed the pitcher of ice water. Still lots of ice, it must've been set there within the last few minutes. Considering how hot the room was, the ice must've been new.

My left arm, hand, leg and foot throbbed. I kind of didn't want to see Mrs. Mattingly anymore. I just wanted to drink lots of water and take a nap. I wasn't even all that curious about who might have written in the diary – hot room equals new entry.

Joe rubbed my head like I was some kid out on a ball field. Then he took the wheelchair and left in a flash. Nana moved to the closet and took out my notebooks. She handed me the one Mrs. Mattingly had given me so I could take notes. Then she gave the diary to Mrs. Mattingly. She opened it to the page with the letter from Stephen.

Mrs. Mattingly said, "Your Nana tells me you had contact from someone who died just hours before. That's pretty crazy. Are you ok about it?"

I gulped down my second cup of water and said, "Well, except for the part that I'm heart-broken that he died. Yeah, I guess it hadn't occurred to me that it's strange to be communicated with by the newly dead. I'm getting used to hearing more from dead people than I do from the living." Then I asked, "Does it seem odd to you?"

Mrs. Mattingly looked out from under her ball cap and said, "I was convinced you, or someone near you, did all the ghost writing. Having someone write that isn't famous or easy to know the background for – it makes this all seem more like magic."

I thought about my new t-shirt, so I said, "Magic's just stuff that science hasn't explained yet."

Mrs. Mattingly made a look that said, "I am the least convinced person you will ever meet."

I stared at her realizing what a cute old lady she had become – to me, anyway. I wouldn't mind seeing pictures of her young, dressed in her psychic-reading outfits. But now, grey curls, ball cap and shining green eyes, she looked pretty and sweet. She'd started growing on me.

I smiled and said, "Who is the cynic now, Mrs. Mattingly?" Then I thought I'd ask her something about herself. Maybe let her know I cared about her life too. So, I asked, "Hey, did Roger Clemens make it into the hall of fame?"

She shed a bunch of worry from her face and answered, "No he did not. Not yet! I guess I was right on that one, wasn't I, Miss Smarty Pants?"

"That's Your Ladyship from now on, Mrs. Mattingly." I winked at Nana and she winked back.

Then I copped a serious tone, "I know you can help Paul come to terms with Stephen's loss. But first I need you to do a reading for me."

"For you?" Mrs. Mattingly looked surprised. "Why you?"

I told her it spooked me a little to have a man dependent on my connection with his late husband. And that I had a question in my mind about some people I cared about. I told her I didn't want to get into it right then.

"Ah Hah!" She exclaimed. "See, you **are** set back a little by hearing from someone who just died. You think it's because they've given you a task to do. But Doud told you to let your mom read the diary and that didn't spook you."

I waved my hand at her as if to say, "Whatever. Let's get on with it."

Mrs. Mattingly reached into her handbag and pulled out her tarot cards wrapped in the silk scarf. She handed them to me, and I cut them six times and handed them back to her.

She turned over the first card. We'd seen that card before. It was the Tower Card. The Tower, broken, people falling from the windows. The card that scared me the first time. Now it didn't scare me at all. I looked over at Mrs. Mattingly and re-alized nothing felt scary anymore.

Mrs. Mattingly commented, "People have changes in their lives. Sometimes people die. This change card could be about Paul's husband, Stephen, dying. Or it could be someone fur-ther in the past. Someone else dying. But not in the future.

No one dying in the future."

"Mrs. Mattingly, it seems my life is consumed by dead people from the past. Is this one of them?" I asked.

Me and dead people. Here we go again. Nothing too psychic there.

She said she didn't know for sure, but she didn't think so. She said it's Stephen or someone else who died in the past and the loss is still felt by someone I care about.

The second card was the King of Cups.

"Ahh." Mrs. Mattingly cooed, "This man was loved very much. This man represents someone that no one will get over losing."

Nana whispered, "That poor man. Poor, poor Paul."

"Or not Paul," Mrs. Mattingly contradicted. "I mean, yes, his husband loved him. But this man is someone near and dear to Genevieve, I think."

Next, she turned over The Devil inverted.

"Oh man," I groaned. "That's the devil, isn't it? And he's upside down."

"There are times we want to act out, Genevieve. Sometimes we want to lash out because things haven't gone our way. We can do something little, like be rude to a stranger. Or we can do something big, the way Stephen stood up to the bully who poisoned his dog." Mrs. Mattingly looked serious when she told me this, "Sometimes you have to let things go. Let the law take care of it."

I asked her, "So Paul needs to let this go?"

She paused for a minute and said, "Yeah. Everyone needs to let everything go." I piped up, "You're talking about Mrs. Welch now, I think."

Mrs. Mattingly asked me what I meant. I waved my good arm, "It doesn't matter."

Then she turned over one last card. There sat the Wheel of Fortune. "Everything's changing. Life goes on. Keep on keeping on. I don't think this message is for you, Genevieve. You know life's changing better than anyone. All kids know life's constantly changing because they are constantly changing. Adults lose track of this message. Let go, move on. Make peace with the past."

I was pretty sure she meant Mrs. Welch now. I didn't mention it. Instead I said, "Yeah, I think you need to do that reading for Paul. He needs to hear these things."

Mrs. Mattingly packed up her cards and she said, "I don't think I could ever pull that reading again if my life depended on it. There were three major Arcana cards. Three out of four cards. But Major Arcana cards are outnumbered in a Tarot deck. I don't know how that happened – except for it being a message meant just for you."

Well, Mrs. Mattingly says let it go. Jack Ruby – one of the world's most famous murderers – says the same thing.

The psychic says let it go because things are always changing anyway. The murderer says let it go because – well – it's none of my business.

Besides, says me, I'll never know the truth.

I know one truth. I am not writing these entries. I never heard of secret CIA rat cancer studies and I wouldn't have known where to look it up.

I admit it. I didn't know Charlie Chaplin wrote that Nat King Cole song I love either. But at least I might have looked that up.

I'm 14. I'm writing in my diary. And I have cancer. I'm not asking questions about cancer though. I'm not thinking about throwing up. I'm not thinking about side effects. I'm the least cancer patient/cancer kid I've ever met. My mind is off my condition and onto science, peace, medicine, love: I spent my time wondering where all the dead guys' posts are coming from.

Mom seems better. Mom, Nana, Mrs. Mattingly: they are all totally copasetic with me and my diary. Why shouldn't they be? It sure takes your mind off other things.

Injecting cancer into somebody. That's cold. I don't think Jack Ruby wanted me to feel sorry for him. But I do. I feel sorry for him and Lee Oswald and that DA. I looked him up. He died at 70 years of age. Natural causes. But never knowing the truth.

Maybe he's like me and this diary. He knew what he believed to be true. Nothing else mattered.

Dr. Borlasa came in a little while ago. I snapped at her because she interrupted me while I read Jack Ruby's letter. I'm nuts about this diary. I'm freaking a little because I only have a few pages left. What happens when the notebook's full? Will people just stop writing?

Dr. Borlasa expected me to be happier about her news, I think. She's sending me home tomorrow. I get my last chemo tonight and I'll continue physical therapy at home. I asked if

Joe would come to my house. Dr. Borlasa said, "No. Joe's an inpatient physical therapist. But he pushed back a little when we mentioned that you'd be leaving soon. So, we allowed him to choose your in-home care giver, some guy he went to Hopkins with. He said you'll love him."

Then she looked at me with a puzzled expression, "You do want to go home, don't you? Back to school?" I nodded yes. I didn't want to admit that I have more friends in the hospital.

"Get some rest, Genevieve," Dr. Borlasa moved toward the doorway. "Mrs. Welch will be here tonight, and then you're leaving bright and early in the morning."

Two phlebotomy techs came in for more blood. "A yick and a stick." Here's hoping those cancer cells are gone when the lab techs look in their microscope.

I don't think I want to write fairy tales anymore. I think I want to keep living them, instead.

I need to quit writing and save the few papers for whoever might visit me on my last night. Besides, once Mrs. Welch reads this book. I'll be lucky if she gives it back.

Mrs. Welch left before I came back up from the chemo lab. She left me this note on top of the diary. I guess she decided not to take up any space in here either. I'll stick the note in this book, so I don't lose it. I sure didn't expect a response like this.

D ear Genevieve,

Thanks for letting me read your "Magic Diary." I'm pretty impressed by all the amazing creativity. I hesitate to comment further, because I don't want to sound like an old fuddy duddy. But this is not what I expected when I gave you the notebook.

I guess I'm glad you managed to express yourself and your feelings about your parents. The early part of the diary is written the way I thought you'd write. But these comments from "the past." I don't think they are a very healthy use of your time. I'm genuinely shocked that someone has used your diary to advance an agenda of some kind.

Genevieve, even if I agreed with everything I read in here, I don't know that this belongs in the hands of a young girl with so much on her mind. I don't know which interfering adult took it on themselves to manipulate this book I gave you. But I, for one – and maybe I'm the only one – am not amused.

Diary aside, I am relieved you are feeling so much better, that you had no kidney damage, and you are on the mend.

Your grandmother told me you'd be back in school by Thursday. I'll see you then.

Best wishes,
Mrs. Welch

Well, she may not have wanted to be a fuddy-duddy but she sure was. I hope she never mentions the diary again. Because I love it and I don't want to defend it to her.

I showed the note to Nana. Nana's miffed at her right now. Looks like she's going to "Teach her a thing or two." Nana, remember what the psychic said, "Let it go."

G ood morning, Genevieve,

I noticed you had trouble falling asleep last night. Excited to go home? I don't think so. More **anxious** to see who would be your last messenger. I almost couldn't stay long enough to write to you. Your insomnia almost ate up all the time I had.

Lucky for me, sleep overtook you. And now I'm here.

My name is Evie. It's short for Evelyn. That's my daughter's middle name too. But you call her Mrs. Welch.

You **probably won't** show her this diary ever again, anyway. But you might not want to tell her I came by, either. I'm sure she wouldn't approve.

I know you love my daughter, and I'm sorry she turned all "bad cop" on you once she read your notebook. She expected the diary to help you make time pass. She had no intention of any real magic happening in it.

My daughter has the sweetest disposition, but sometimes she can get very grumpy. She's religious. The idea of dead people writing to you upsets her sensibilities. Even if one of the ghostwriters is a saint!

My grumpy kid carries a lot of blame around. She pretty much blames my second husband for everything in her life that's made her sad. She's a great person, but she's lived through tragedy and it's made her less willing to take the flights of fancy a book like this requires.

When she was just a little bit older than you, I swallowed a bottle of medicine and never woke up again. I spent five days in the hospital THIS HOSPITAL before they disconnected the life support machines, and I passed away from her.

Wow, she got mad. She got mad at me at first, but that passed rather quickly. She got a notebook like yours and she wrote all her feelings down. She poured her anger and her hurt into that book. It seemed to help her cope.

I can't help but think she expected your magic diary to be like hers. A coping mechanism. A place to write your angry thoughts about your cancer. The same way she had written her angry thoughts about my death.

My husband, her stepfather, found her diary. He did a bad thing. Perhaps an irresistible thing. But something he shouldn't have done. He read it.

My husband saw how she blamed him for my death. He learned that she hated him and wanted him to die instead of me. She resented him for not donating my organs so that other people could live on with little bits of her mother inside them. Especially my heart. She wanted my heart to beat on even if I couldn't use it anymore.

Genevieve, it wasn't Wallace's fault. It was mine.

I had amyotrophic lateral sclerosis. It's not as common in women. You know it by another name. Most folks call it Lou Gehrig's disease. Lou Gehrig played baseball better than just about any other player in the world, until this disease took his muscle control away from him. He played 2130 consecutive games until ALL forced him to retire at 36. He was dead by 38.

On July 4, 1939, Lou Gehrig took a few minutes to tell a packed Yankee Stadium how he felt about his life. Lou told his spellbound audience, "Fans, for the past two weeks you have been reading about the bad break I got. Yet today I consider myself the luckiest man on the face of the earth."

He went on to praise the guys he played ball with and then his comments turned more personal. He thanked the ordinary people in his life, "When you have a wonderful mother-in-law who takes sides with you in squabbles with her own daughter - that's something. When you have a father and a mother who work all their lives so you can have an education and build your body - it's a blessing. When you have a wife, who has been a tower of strength and shown more courage than you dreamed existed - that's the finest I know."

Genevieve, I read about Lou Gehrig's courage and the courage required from everyone who loved him. I knew I didn't have that courage. ALL is a terrible way to die. Patients choke to death because the muscles in the throat stop working. I didn't want to die that way. I didn't want my daughter to see me die that way.

The only one who knew the truth, the only one who knew I

was dying anyway, was my dear sweet Wallace. Wallace tried to convince me to include my daughter in my decision. He said she would respect me and my wishes. He told me she wouldn't want me to suffer either.

I couldn't do it. I begged Wallace not to tell her EVER that I had taken the coward's way out. Genevieve, he never did. He didn't tell anyone that my organs carried that deadly disease and couldn't be donated. He kept quiet about everything and let my daughter and the rest of my family blame him. Now she hates him. She won't see him.

At least not on purpose.

But I know you know by now, my daughter ran into Wallace in your intensive care room the other day. She hates him. Blames him. Thinks I killed myself to get away from him.

I think I made the wrong decision not to tell her about my disease. But Wallace won't go back on his word. I died in early spring. My daughter went to live with my sister, Debbie, in Spokane.

Wallace finished the school year teaching modern U.S. history at Central High School and never went back. He took his teaching pension early, paid my daughter's way through college by sending the money to Debbie. Debbie didn't hate him, but she also never knew the truth, so she honored my daughter's wishes and never mentioned Wallace again.

Once Wallace retired from teaching, he took the job here cleaning rooms overnights. He thinks it brings him closer to me when he helps other people who get sick.

He's a good man. I'm glad he's taken such good care of you this past week and a half. Perhaps you can stay friends.

Best of luck dear Genevieve. Keep being courageous. And thanks for loving my daughter. She's a great kid who doesn't always make the right choices. I guess she got that trait from me.

Lots of love, Evie

Evie, you didn't leave me much room to write here. But I guess I don't need much. I will never get mad again at Mrs. Welch for dissing my diary. It wasn't ever about me anyway, I guess. It was always about her.

Boy, Jack Ruby called it. People have so many secrets.

Wallace came in as I packed my things into my book bag. He said the nurse asked him to turn down the heat. He pulled the key from his key ring and unlocked the thermostat.

Wallace didn't just come in to adjust the temperature: he'd brought me a suitcase. He said he looked everywhere for the LL Bean one with the wig stand but couldn't find it. I guess Wallace never got over the urge to read other people's diaries.

I thanked him and loaded my clothes into it and my books – all but this one – into my book bag. I asked him if he had any messages for Mrs. Welch. His smile fell to a frown and he mumbled a painfilled, "No."

I probably shouldn't have asked him that.

I changed the subject. I said, "Thanks again for the suitcase. I hope I never have to bring it back here."

"Me too," he said, and that wonderful smile came back.

I hugged him and asked him one last question, "Do you miss teaching U.S. history?" He winked and said, "Sometimes."

Afterward

1987 I gave birth to my second child. Twenty-six years old, excited to bring a new baby home to my 18-month-old daughter, Becky, I had a sweet little guy named John. In those days no one knew the gender of their child prearrival. When asked what someone wanted, everyone responded, "Ten fingers and ten toes: just a healthy baby." Unfortunately, that isn't always the result. In the first few hours of John's life, no one knew what was wrong. In the first few moments, I didn't know anything was wrong. Labor and delivery can be chaotic events. When the nurses whisked John out of the room, I had no idea they left to make frantic phone calls, x-ray his back and alert our pediatrician to get to the hospital on the double. I'll never forget the doctor walking into my room where my sister, daughter, and I cradled John between us. He said he'd scheduled a specialist to see the baby because he couldn't be sure what we were up against.

My sister, Claire, asked, "How upset should Patty be?" The doctor responded, "Well, if she cried all night, I wouldn't blame her." I proceeded to cry all night – as instructed.

After three years of watching, worrying and waiting for John to grow big enough to withstand a radical reconstruction of his back, Dr. John McGill of Bangor, Maine, turned off the ticking time bomb aimed at my son's life. My very first thank you of this book goes to Dr. McGill.

Thank you. Aren't those the words used when someone passes the salt? Thank you doesn't seem enough. Every day my son got better. Started walking again. Put this chapter behind him. Gratitude haunted me.

Within a couple of years, the hospital where John's life changing surgery occurred had an opening for a public relations professional to raise public awareness and help the hospital save more kids like John.

I became the director of the hospital's annual telethon campaign. I became their yearlong pediatric public relations coordinator. We raised money through a national affiliate to help ill and injured children. For the next few years I worked directly with kids and the medical professionals that struggled to make them healthy. I knew their doctors, their nurses, their housekeepers, their parents, their grandparents, their siblings, and their teachers. I knew their routines. I travelled the country with them. I sat by their side as they prepped for procedures and I encouraged them as they prepared to go on TV.

As time wore on, my pockets filled with the pictures of courageous children: some who got well and others who didn't. I went to fundraisers. I raised the money for expensive medical procedures insurance wouldn't cover. I attended funerals.

One of the remarkable children I met, Arian Hagkerdar, inspired this book. Genevieve – the hero of this novel – embodies so many of Arian's loving stellar qualities, but she still can't do that kid justice. Arian was funny, smart, adorable and twelve when she died of Acute Lymphoblastic Leukemia. No, she didn't have a magic diary, but just about every other aspect of that kid was magic.

I loved her and I miss her still.

The rest of the characters in this book are my own creations. The stories of the events that happened to the kids on the eighth floor are real as I remember them. But Arian's mom and grand mom – great women that they are – are not the women in this book.

There was no psychic. For the psychic inspiration I have to thank Marakay Rogers, a great legal mind, a great friend, and as I would come to learn, a great Tarot Card reader. I appreciate her psychic patience. Marakay took my random phone calls – although perhaps she knew they were coming! She allowed me to describe a scene in the book, and then instructed me which cards my psychic would pull for the reading.
Marakay Rogers breathed an extra-terrestrial wisdom into Mrs. Mattingly's character.

The journalists out of history, the ghostwriters, did the things I said they did – with the one exception of coming back from the dead. I'm afraid I made that part up. I love doing research and the folks who visit with Genevieve, via her diary, are some of my favorite people in history.

As an historian it's no surprise I picked Truman or Eisen-hower – I studied them extensively in grad school at the University of Amsterdam. I included Mother Seton because she reminds me of Mary Jean Horna, a good and faithful woman who quietly helps homeless children. All the other ghosts are pretty self-explanatory.

I took special joy in interviewing Paul H. LaMarche PhD, my brother, nuclear physicist and a Vice Provost at Princeton University. I called him one day and said, "Can you take a few minutes to answer a couple of questions?" He said, "Sure, what's up?" I said, "I'm working on a book, so could you pre-tend to be Albert Einstein when you answer?"

His answer was pure Einstein, he said, "Sure, but can't you find anyone smarter?" We both laughed. But seriously, no I couldn't. Paul's that smart.

When John turned 12 or 13, I told him I wanted to write this book. He told me, "You better make the reader fall in love with that kid or they'll never hang on long enough to meet your historic figures." I hope I have made Genevieve lovable. I sure love her. That's why I named her after my mom.

Once John gave me permission to bare my soul as a mom of a kid with a congenital anomaly, I sat down and wrote the first 60 or so pages of this book. Then I got busy. For nearly twenty years the book sat waiting for me.

During my career as a broadcaster, one of my listeners wrote to me wanting to help kids and adults with healthcare chal-lenges. So we did. She became one of my best friends. Theresa Savage loved the idea of this book. She would ask me once a year or so when I was going to finish and I'd tell her, "When I have time." Sure that I would lose what I'd already written, Theresa offered to hold it for safe keeping. A couple of years ago, she gave it back to me.

In 2017, I quit working full time and sat down to finish this, my first novel. I never would have been able to do so if not for my darling husband, Chad Bruce. He didn't know the story, but he believed in me. I read him each section as I completed it and he cried through most of them. I never dreamed I'd have such an able champion. He has made the dream of the Magic Diary come true.

If not for the continual encouragement of mystery writer and dear friend, JM West, the Magic Diary wouldn't be in your hands right now.

If not for the wisdom of my editor, Chris Fenwick, it wouldn't be as fun to read.

The last folks named who made this possible are also the first: the children of the eighth floor. I worked with them to show my gratitude for my own son's life and only became more grateful in the process. Those children, their love, their courage, their joy – in the face of circumstances that bring most adults to their knees – taught me every precept I ever needed to learn. And I hope that I have come close to relating those lessons here.

ABOUT THE AUTHOR

Pat LaMarche, an award-winning broadcaster and journalist, has spent a lifetime traveling around the world and across the nation telling the tales of ordinary folks living through unimaginable hardship. Her two non-fiction books, *Left Out in America* and *Daddy, What's the Middle Class?*, exposed the harsh realities of life for the impoverished American and their ongoing struggle to survive. Frustrated by a lack of change, this social justice warrior stepped out in front of the pen and microphone to run for office and change things herself. In 2004, LaMarche took on both Dick Cheney and John Edwards as the Green Party's vice-presidential candidate.

Fascinated by history, LaMarche and her children lived in Europe while she pursued a graduate degree at the University of Amsterdam. LaMarche's first novel, *Magic Diary*, combines her passion for learning with her keen insight into the American healthcare system.

71127945R00116

Made in the USA
Middletown, DE
29 September 2019